W9-CNG-418

Cold Hearted

A Tale of the Wicked Stepmother

Cold Hearted

A Tale of the Wicked Stepmother

By Serena Valentino

Disney • Hyperion
Los Angeles • New York

Adapted in part from the Disney film *Cinderella*.

First Hardcover Edition, June 2021
10 9 8 7 6 5 4 3 2 1
FAC-020093-21169
Printed in the United States of America

Designed by Phil T. Buchanan
This book is set in 13-point Garamond 3 LT Pro.

Library of Congress Cataloging-in-Publication Data

Names: Valentino, Serena, author.
Title: Cold hearted : a tale of the wicked stepmother / by Serena Valentino.
Description: First hardcover edition. • Los Angeles : Disney Hyperion, 2021. • Series: Villains • "Adapted in part from the Disney film *Cinderella*"—Copyright page. • Audience: Ages 12–18. • Audience: Grades 7–9. • Summary: Fairy Godmother is reluctant to help Queen Cinderella's evil stepmother and stepsisters until she sees their story from a different perspective.
Identifiers: LCCN 2020036702 • ISBN 9781368025287 (hardcover)
Subjects: CYAC: Fairy tales.
Classification: LCC PZ8.V23525 Co 2021 • DDC [Fic]—dc23
LC record available at https://lccn.loc.gov/2020036702

Reinforced binding
www.DisneyBooks.com

Dedicated to Rich Thomas: Without your encouragement and guidance, and that of the many other talented people I have worked with at Disney over the years, I would have never written this series. You will always have my heartfelt gratitude.

CHAPTER I

THE BOOK OF FAIRY TALES

The Tremaines

Not too long ago and rather far away, but still within the Many Kingdoms, there was a moldering old château. This château had two distinguishing attributes: the first and most remarkable was that Cinderella, the queen of her land, once called this strange, foreboding place her home. The second was that it was the subject of wild rumors—that it was haunted by Lady Tremaine and her two daughters.

The lady's daughters, Anastasia and Drizella, were said to roam the château in white dresses, and the specter of the lady was said to have been seen talking with the ghost of her beloved cat, Lucifer, as she lamented the loss of her one true love.

The rumors told a tragic ghost tale, filled with misery and deception. But the truth was far more interesting. The fact was, the lady and her daughters were very much alive, despite their wraithlike appearance, and they were indeed trapped within the old crumbling château with no hope of escape. You see, unlike Cinderella, the Tremaine sisters did not have a fairy godmother to look after them.

We probably don't have to tell you about Cinderella's past, before she became queen, back when she lived with the Tremaines. If you picked up this book, then you are already well acquainted with Cinderella's story, but just in case you've been living outside the Many Kingdoms, and you have somehow managed to go a lifetime without hearing Cinderella's story, I suppose it best I tell you a little bit about her family.

Like most princesses in the Many Kingdoms, this poor girl lost her mother at a young age, and it was left to her father to find a proper stepmother to make a happy home for his daughter. It seems the lives of mothers in the Many Kingdoms are often cut short, and the stepmothers who replace them are almost always cruel and selfish creatures, but that is a story for another time. We could speculate that something supernatural was at work in the Many Kingdoms, or that the blame should almost certainly be placed on the widowers' poor choices in stepmothers. One might even argue that the lives of these women were predestined by the prevailing misguided notion in fairy circles that all stepmothers are evil.

Cinderella's father didn't think much beyond the care of his daughter when he chose his new wife, aside from making sure she was a lady from a good family, well respected in her community, and that she had a large dowry. This lady seemed like the perfect choice, really. She was a stately-looking woman, still rather handsome, and most importantly she had a fortune of her own, which of course would become his upon their marriage. This was, and remains to this day, a rather unfortunate and antiquated custom in the Many Kingdoms: all of a woman's possessions become property of her husband upon marriage. But this didn't concern the lady. She thought the young girl's father to be very handsome, with a title far greater than her own, what she assumed was a substantial fortune, and a beautiful home in which she could raise her own children alongside his daughter.

However, this lady's hopes for the marriage went beyond practical concerns. She sincerely loved this man and looked forward to having a beautiful life with him, even if she didn't say so when he was courting her. He seemed like the sort of man who desired a pragmatic woman, and the lady was indeed very sensible and far too proper to mention such things. She prided herself on her stoicism.

But we'll get to that part of the story soon. For now we'll concern ourselves with the lady's unfortunate daughters, who have been withering away within the confines of their home, under the watchful eye of their domineering mother. The situation attracted the attention of their stepsister, Queen Cinderella, who found she couldn't ignore her stepsisters' sad circumstances.

My dearest Fairy Godmother,

I am so sorry to have learned the Fairylands have been in a state of turmoil, and though I do not wish to trouble you at such a time, I must write to you about a gravely important matter that has me in great distress.

You see, my stepsisters, Anastasia and Drizella, are in a desperate situation, and for reasons you understand all too well, I am unable to help them. If the Fairylands can spare you, won't you please come to me as soon as you are able? Drizella, Anastasia, and I need your help.

Sincerely,

Queen Cinderella

The Fairy Godmother crumpled up the letter from Queen Cinderella, which took great effort since it was rather large and written on the sturdy parchment used for official royal correspondence.

"Honestly, I don't know what Cinderella is thinking! What in the Fairylands are we supposed to do about Anastasia and Drizella? The fairies are not in the business of helping the likes of them!"

The Fairy Godmother's wings twitched violently as she waited for her sister to respond.

Of course, the Fairy Godmother's sister, Nanny, wasn't listening to her. Lately, Nanny had been in the Fairylands much more often than usual. She had spent many years on her own adventures, only recently deciding to return to help her sister when the fairies were in great peril. But that is another story, one that you can find in the book of fairy tales. This story finds the sister fairies in the Fairy Godmother's blossoming garden, where they were just sitting down for their afternoon tea when they were interrupted by the queen's message.

"Cinderella is your charge. You have to go to her. She's asked you for your help!" said Nanny, giving the Fairy Godmother a withering look. The Fairy Godmother had always thought that her sister would be more pleasant to be around if she smiled more often. Nanny had silver ringlets and sparkling eyes. She was a round, cute little woman, with powdery soft skin that felt like vellum paper. She was far older than the Fairy Godmother and used it to her advantage as often as it pleased her, including bossing the Fairy Godmother around.

The Fairy Godmother tapped her wand on the edge of the table, agitated, as her sister went on. They were in *her* garden, after all, and Nanny was fussing at her, *as usual*.

"Aren't you the least bit interested why Cinderella is so upset? Something awful must have happened to Anastasia and Drizella to have her so worried. And you *are* fairy duty–bound to go to Cinderella if she calls you. I don't think this is something you can ignore," said Nanny in her usual superior fashion, which the Fairy Godmother had grown to detest even more now that her sister had been spending so much time in the Fairylands.

The Fairy Godmother was still recovering her nerves since their latest ordeal. They had just survived an attack in Fairyland by the Odd Sisters. And before that an attack by Maleficent.

"Here we are, hardly able to catch our breath after the near destruction of the Fairylands at the hands of your old charges, the Odd Sisters, and now you're trying to drag us into another battle. I can't go flying here and there just because Cinderella is worried about her stepsisters. They're not fairy-worthy," the Fairy Godmother said. Her hands shook as she poured herself a cup of tea to calm her nerves. She hated being so rattled by all this, especially in front of her sister, but she couldn't help it. From the moment she'd received the letter from Cinderella pleading for help, her heart had not stopped fluttering. She was now regretting sharing the news with Nanny.

"Well, I don't see you have any other choice! Cinderella has asked for your help, and it's your job to do just that! And why exactly are you so rattled by the Tremaines? They're non-magical and hardly a threat," said Nanny, eyeing her sister in a way the Fairy Godmother hated.

The Fairy Godmother cleared her throat, steeled her nerves, and spoke in the slowest, sternest voice she could muster. "I will not help Anastasia and Drizella, and that is the last word on this topic,

Nanny. Now, if you'd like to continue having our tea, I'd appreciate it if we could talk about something else. The subject of Cinderella and her wicked stepsisters is closed." The Fairy Godmother took a sip of her tea and put her teacup down gently on the saucer, never taking her eyes off Nanny. "Besides," she continued, "I know what this is really about. You feel guilty about everything the Odd Sisters have done, not to mention the sacrifice Circe had to make to stop them from destroying the Many Kingdoms."

Nanny looked as though the Fairy Godmother had slapped her in the face. She got up from the table abruptly and violently, causing her chair to make a horrible scraping noise on the cobblestones in the Fairy Godmother's garden.

The Fairy Godmother felt terrible. Yes, her sister was annoying, domineering, and rather eccentric for a fairy. (After all, she hated wearing her wings, and only did so begrudgingly at the Fairy Godmother's request. The Fairy Godmother could never fathom it since wings were so glorious and their fairy-given right and honor.) Still, she loved Nanny and felt sorry for bringing up a topic that hurt her.

"Nanny! I'm sorry! Where are you going? I shouldn't have mentioned Circe. I know you're grieving. I am so sorry!" she said, but Nanny didn't answer, and the Fairy Godmother could tell she'd broken her sister's heart, even with her back turned to her. Nanny's wings were hanging low.

The Fairy Godmother knew she should have never brought up *the debacle.* That's what the Fairy Godmother had been calling it. And that's exactly what it was, a debacle. And as far as the Fairy Godmother was concerned, Circe and her mothers, the Odd Sisters, were perfectly fine where they were, in the Place Between, far away from the Fairylands and the Many Kingdoms, where they couldn't hurt anyone. It wasn't her business if Circe chose to go beyond the veil with her mothers, or come back to the land of the living after she said her tearful goodbyes to those horrible witch mothers of hers. This was a matter for witches, not fairies—it was no longer their concern. As long as the Fairylands were safe and as long as the Odd Sisters were as far away from them as possible, she was content. Oh yes, there was some way the ancestors could bring them back if they chose, but the Fairy Godmother felt Circe would make the right choice. For all Circe's failings, the Fairy Godmother thought she was a brave young woman. She had, after all, sacrificed her own life to stop her mothers from destroying the Fairylands. Circe had saved the Many Kingdoms, and for that the fairies would always be grateful. And the Fairy Godmother knew Circe wouldn't make the mistake of bringing the Odd Sisters back into the world again. So as far as she was concerned the matter was put to rest. What they all needed now was to tighten up ranks and make sure nothing like that would ever happen again, even if that meant not entangling the fairies with the likes of the Tremaines. Of course her sister, Nanny, didn't agree, and as usual she was Hades-bent on flying them into the face of danger.

Nanny tutted at the Fairy Godmother (no doubt having read her sister's mind) and turned to face her.

"Sister, please don't ever mention Circe again," Nanny said. "And don't insult me or my intelligence by invoking her name in an attempt to distract me. You know as well as I do that you are fairy duty–bound to help Queen Cinderella!"

As Nanny spoke, the Fairy Godmother grew more and more agitated. She tapped her wand on the edge of the table, causing it to spark in rapid bursts that Nanny had to dodge.

"Sister, stop that!" Nanny scolded. "You know you don't have a choice. You *have* to help Cinderella. And as much as you will hate it, that means you have to help Anastasia and Drizella. I can't believe we are even having this discussion." Nanny was so angry her wings were now standing up straight behind her.

"Don't you dare twitch your wings at me, Nanny!" said the Fairy Godmother, slamming her teacup onto the saucer, then putting her hand to her head dramatically as if her sister was giving her a terrible headache. "Can I please, *just for once*, have my tea in peace without you pestering me with all this wish-granting nonsense? Next thing you know we will be granting wishes to Anastasia and Drizella themselves!"

"Well, sister, that's exactly what I had in mind." Nanny laughed as she got up from the table again and slowly walked away, not bothering to turn back to look at her sister even though she was yelling behind her.

"Don't you walk away from me!" cried the Fairy Godmother. "Where do you think you're going?"

Nanny looked over her shoulder and smiled. "To get my magic mirror. Let's see for ourselves why Cinderella is so worried."

The Fairy Godmother slammed her wand down on the table, snapping it in half with an explosion of glittering sparks. "Oh, look what you made me do! What am I supposed to do now? I can't do magic without my wand! It will take the Maker of Wands weeks to make me another," she screeched, but her sister had already gone into the house.

When Nanny returned she found the Fairy Godmother pacing back and forth, nearly in tears. Nanny rolled her eyes. She waved her hand, effortlessly mending her sister's wand.

"There. Good as new. Now sit down and calm yourself. Let's see why Cinderella is so worried about her sisters." Nanny cast her hand across the mirror. "Show us the Tremaines!"

"Sister, stop!" the Fairy Godmother protested. "I don't want to lay eyes on those creatures. We know everything there is to know about them. Besides, I know exactly what has become of them, and they deserve their fate for what they did to my Cinderella."

Nanny looked into her magic mirror anyway, ignoring her sister, and was shocked by what she saw. Anastasia and Drizella were in a deplorable state. The château was crumbling around them and filled with cats. They were wearing tatty white dresses, and she could hear the voice of Lady Tremaine in the background raving over everything she had lost.

"No wonder you didn't want me to look in on them!" said Nanny, putting down the mirror. "We have to do something about this! This is horrendous! Why hasn't Cinderella done anything to help her sisters?" Nanny was appalled.

"She's bound by magic. I put an enchantment on the Tremaines and Cinderella so they would never meet again," said the Fairy Godmother.

"So the Tremaines are trapped in that house?" Nanny was horrified and felt deeply ashamed for her part in their story. "I had no idea they've been trapped there all these years. If I had known, I would have done something. Oh, this is all my fault. I can't believe we let this happen." Nanny clutched her mirror so tightly the Fairy Godmother thought she would break it.

"Stop it! You're going to hurt yourself," said the Fairy Godmother. "You know as well as I do there was no other choice. Lady Tremaine picked her path even though she was warned."

"But surely we can remove the enchantment so those poor girls can leave that place and Cinderella could help them herself if she wished? I'm just heartsick knowing that they are still there after all these years."

The fact was, the Fairy Godmother could remove the enchantment if she wanted. But why should she? She had thought carefully before placing it, and she had to do what was best for her charge. It was her job to protect Cinderella, and she wasn't about to do anything that would put Cinderella at risk, not now or ever. "I won't do it! I won't ruin Cinderella's happily ever after! Not for those horrible girls or anyone else. Anastasia and Drizella are getting exactly what they deserve!" said the Fairy Godmother, standing up to her sister.

Nanny was unrelenting. "I spent time with them, sister; you didn't. I was their nanny, and I cared for those girls. You have no idea what they've been through. And I feel just awful we didn't help them when we could. Those poor girls don't deserve this!"

"I believe they do," said the Fairy Godmother,

catching sight of her protégées the Three Good Fairies walking down her garden path and about to enter her gate. "The law is very clear when it comes to crimes against princesses-to-be. Anastasia and Drizella, not to mention their tyrannical mother, are lucky they survived their story."

Nanny scoffed. "And how exactly is it determined who is a princess-to-be and who is not? Why weren't Anastasia or Drizella marked as princesses-to-be? Why was their fate written so tragically while Cinderella's was so charmed?"

"Cinderella's life was not charmed! She was tortured by the Tremaines, and they're lucky they got off so easily. Most storybook villains meet a less kind fate. I'm not even sure how we let those three escape their punishment!"

Nanny scoffed. But before she could answer, the Three Good Fairies came bubbling into the garden making themselves quite at home, pouring cups of tea and conjuring little cakes and scones to share.

"What were you fairies chatting about so

animatedly when we got here?" asked Merryweather, conjuring some of her special preserves and honey from her own gardens. But before the Fairy Godmother could answer, Nanny took over the conversation.

"It has come to our attention that the fairies have been holding Lady Tremaine and her daughters captive in Queen Cinderella's old château," said Nanny, her wings fluttering with agitation. "This is highly disturbing considering my connection to the Tremaine family." Nanny wiggled back and forth in her seat, trying to make herself comfortable. The Fairy Godmother thought it was laughable that her sister, who was born a fairy, never felt comfortable in her own wings.

"Come now! I wouldn't put it quite like that, sister!" said the Fairy Godmother, feeling a bit guilty once she heard it in such simple, straightforward terms.

"Good heavens! We can't help those awful girls!" screeched Merryweather, startling Fauna and Flora.

"I'm sorry you're so upset, Nanny, but I have the majority in this. We will not help Anastasia and Drizella. My fairies will never grant wishes to foul demons, witches, evil stepmothers, or cruel stepsisters! Not ever! Not while I'm in charge anyway!" said the Fairy Godmother, feeling very proud of herself.

"Let's not forget you're not in charge of the Fairylands, sister. *I am.*" Nanny's tone was firm. "You stepped down, and Oberon agreed that I should take the lead. Now, I'm going to ask Opal to fly a message to Cinderella letting her know the Fairy Godmother is on her way to help Anastasia and Drizella. Do you want to disappoint her? Or do I have to strip you of your charge and become Cinderella's fairy godmother myself?"

The Three Good Fairies gasped. "You can't do that!"

"Oh yes I can! And I will! Make your choice, sister. Help Queen Cinderella, or I will!" said Nanny.

The Fairy Godmother was hurt deeply by her

sister's threats, but she remained stalwart. She picked up the book of fairy tales, flipping through it until she found Lady Tremaine and her daughters' story. "Nanny, this is nonsense," she said. "You know their story, you were there. And you know as well as I do Lady Tremaine and her horrible daughters didn't even need the encouragement of those meddlesome Odd Sisters! They treated my poor Cinderella reprehensibly on their own accord. It's all in the book of fairy tales that Snow White sent back to us after *the ordeal*."

Nanny smiled, and her sister didn't like it. She knew that meant she was up to something.

"Okay, sister. Let's read their story, then. Perhaps there will be no redemption for Lady Tremaine, but I wager even you will want to help her daughters after reading their tale. Remember I was there, and more importantly, I know your heart."

Fauna, Flora, and Merryweather had been silent, waiting to see what the Fairy Godmother would say. They had been dumbstruck by Nanny's earlier comments and had been sitting there the entire time, jaws dropped.

"Merryweather, close your mouth. A dragonfly is going to fly into it!" said the Fairy Godmother. "And magic us some more refreshments." Then she snapped at Fauna, "And you! Send a message to the Blue Fairy. Tell her there is an emergency Fairy Council meeting and she's needed immediately." Finally, she looked to Nanny. "Where is the King of the Fairies? Do you think he'd like to sit on the council meeting?"

Nanny laughed, no doubt because her sister was still acting as though she was in charge of the Fairylands. "Oberon is at Morningstar Castle with Princess Tulip preparing for another of their adventures. But I am sure he's listening," said Nanny.

The Fairy Godmother knew that even if he wasn't listening, Nanny would fill him in later. They had been closer than ever, which sent a tingling rage through her body, but she had to put that aside for now. "All right, then," she said. "Once Blue Fairy arrives we will read Lady Tremaine's story, and *the council* will decide if we should help Drizella and Anastasia."

"I think that sounds fair," said Nanny, with a suspicious look on her face that the Fairy Godmother didn't like. But she decided it was a victory anyway. She knew in her heart her fairies would never agree to help Anastasia and Drizella, no matter what Nanny had up her sleeve.

CHAPTER II

THE FAIRY COUNCIL

Once the entire council had gathered, the Fairy Godmother took out the book of fairy tales. "Very well, then," she said. "If no one objects, we will read Lady Tremaine's story, and perhaps my sister, Nanny, here will finally stop pestering me to help those monstrous girls Anastasia and Drizella once and for all." She winked to her favorite fairy trio, knowing they wouldn't let her down.

Lady Tremaine

London may be far away, but we have found ways for our magic to reach beyond the Many Kingdoms, even into the drawing rooms of unsuspecting fancy lords and ladies. Take Cruella de Vil, for example. Even though her tale was written in her own voice, who do you think inspired her to write it?

But this isn't Cruella's story. It's Lady Tremaine's.

Lady Tremaine lost her husband early in their marriage and was left to care for their two young daughters on her own. Unlike most women in her circumstances, Lady Tremaine was well provided for. Upon his death her stately lord of a husband left her a great fortune. That, combined with the fortune she herself had brought to the marriage, meant she was quite a wealthy woman.

The lady of the house had everything she desired, except for one thing: her true love. She had lost him far too soon. What she did have, however, was a house full of servants: nannies, governesses, parlor maids, cooks, a butler, pantry boys, boot boys, footmen, scullery maids, housemaids, a head housemaid, and of course her lady's maid, the elderly Mrs. Bramble. Lady Tremaine treated her servants well and with respect, and insisted her daughters Anastasia and Drizella do the same. The household staff doted on them. The Tremaines and their staff lived comfortably in their lavish London town house. It was always full and bustling with activity, so Lady Tremaine didn't feel quite so alone. She enjoyed giving her daughters the best life possible.

Like most aristocratic Londoners, the Tremaines flitted to and from the country like birds, going hither and thither as the season dictated. One fateful day, the lady was about to embark on such a trip, unaware that it would forever alter the course of her life. We wonder what would have happened to Lady Tremaine and her daughters had Lady Tremaine decided not to visit her old friend Lady Prudence Hackle, but then again once it's written in the book of fairy tales there is little one can do to change one's fate.

Before the flurry of the day took hold that morning, Lady Tremaine sat in the front parlor, making time for a repose before her daughters woke or her maids came to her with questions about what to pack for their trip to the country. The front parlor had been one of her favorite rooms when her husband had been alive. They spent many quiet moments there, enjoying their coffee in the mornings, or sipping drinks after a night out, or just sitting in their own corners of the room enjoying a good book. She was missing those days more keenly than usual and found that in the silence of that morning she could almost feel her husband with her.

It was a bright, sunny parlor with large French doors that opened onto a balcony with a breathtaking view of the city. She loved the sounds of the city bustling below and would sit for hours listening to musicians playing on the corner, always making sure to have one of the boot boys take some money down to thank them for entertaining her.

Like almost every other morning, the lady went to her desk, took a few coins from her drawer, and pulled the cord that hung to the left of the fireplace. It called her butler, Mr. Avery, who had been in her household for years. He had been there when her husband was still alive, and she felt that in a strange way he had taken her husband's place. At least in that he was always there to care for her. Avery was a

tall, lanky, stoic man, with black hair distinguished by a white streak on the left side. His face was heavily lined, almost like chiseled rock, and his eyes were deep brown.

"Good morning, Lady Tremaine," he said when he entered the room, making her smile. She knew he wouldn't return the gesture. He was too austere, too serious, and far too busy for things like smiling. Lady Tremaine was almost sure Avery's pants could catch fire and he would never let on, if he could possibly avoid it. That was just the sort of man he was.

"Good morning, Avery. Could you please have one of the boot boys take these coins down to those musicians on the corner? And have Daisy bring me my coffee."

Avery narrowed his eyes at his lady but said nothing.

"Do you disapprove, Avery?" she asked, already knowing what he would say. They'd had several variations of this conversation before, and it was one of the chief reasons she felt Avery sometimes

took her husband's place. He, like her husband, was a man who preferred things done by the book. And ladies didn't do things like send coins down to musicians who performed on corners.

"It is not for me to approve or disapprove, my lady," he said, taking the coins from Lady Tremaine, and then adding, "Oh, and, my lady, Nanny Pinch was wondering if she could bring the girls to see you this morning rather than this afternoon."

Lady Tremaine sighed. "Oh yes, they will be out shopping this afternoon, I forgot. Yes, yes, tell Nanny Pinch to bring them if she must. But, Avery, please wait to do so until after I've had my coffee. You're probably the only person alive I can abide talking to before I've had my coffee," she said, laughing.

"Yes, my lady," he replied, and left the room. The lady laughed to herself again, wondering if she would ever get the man to crack a smile. It had become her personal mission, to make Avery smile.

She took her rose-colored shawl from the back

of her chair, draped it around her shoulders, and sat on the red velvet couch. The room had felt so lonely since her husband had passed away more than six years ago, and she wondered why she still used it as the family room after he was gone. She supposed it was out of habit. All the ladies she knew used their front parlors in this way. This was where the ladies of the house spent their mornings, greeted their children, or entertained their closest friends. Larger gatherings were of course held in grander rooms, but Lady Tremaine hadn't held a large gathering since her husband was alive.

These days the lady attended parties at the houses of others. She was besieged by invitations after her husband died. Well-meaning and thoughtful invitations meant to distract her from her grief. But now that so much time had passed she was starting to long for the days when she was the one to throw the party, and she missed having someone to walk up the stairs with after the last party guest left, and someone to chat with over breakfast about their plans for the day, or in the evening after going to the opera. She wondered if it wasn't time to consider finding a new companion. A new husband.

When she woke up that morning she hadn't expected this was something that would cross her mind, but as she sat on the red couch in her parlor, she felt she might at last be ready to fall in love again.

"Ah, Daisy," said the lady, looking at the sweet-faced little maid who brought in the coffee. She was hardly more than a girl, with sparkling eyes and small, delicate features that reminded Lady Tremaine of a little mouse. "Please put the coffee there. Thank you, Daisy." The maid placed the coffee service on a small round table in front of her. It was Lady Tremaine's favorite coffee set, black with gold trim.

"Cook would like to know if you wanted breakfast this morning, my lady," Daisy asked timidly.

Lady Tremaine laughed. Her cook, Mrs. Prattle, prompted her maids to ask this every morning knowing full well what her answer would be.

"Please tell Mrs. Prattle just to send something up for the girls in the schoolroom if she hasn't already. And we will want a packed lunch for our journey to the country." The lady smiled at the mouse of a maid.

"Yes, my lady; she already has a hamper packed for you and the girls." She quickly corrected herself, "I mean for Miss Drizella and Miss Anastasia."

Lady Tremaine wondered what types of women her servants had worked for before coming to her household. Of course, she wanted the staff to be sensible, diligent, and respectful, but she didn't insist on unnecessary formalities. Not when they were alone, at any rate. Oh sure, when her husband was alive they would throw lavish parties, and she'd always liked giving her lord and lady friends a good show with all the proper formalities from time to time. And of course she had an air of reserve when speaking to her friends' servants, which was to be expected. But she always left a little something for them at the end of their stay. She wondered if her friends were like this, too. She wondered if they weren't all just putting on a show. Perhaps when they were alone they were more real with their servants. Treated them like people, talked to them, asked them about their days, and smiled at them. She hoped they did.

It made her feel less lonely to have so many servants about the house. She had no illusions about them being actual friends, but there was no reason not to be friendly. "Thank you, Daisy. You can tell Nanny Pinch she may bring the girls in now if she likes, unless Avery has already done so. I'm sure he has other things to attend to for our trip. And, Daisy, I will tell Avery that he's to arrange a little outing for the staff who aren't coming along with me," said Lady Tremaine.

"Yes, my lady." Daisy left the room with a smile. Lady Tremaine had known the news of an outing would bring a smile to Daisy's face, but then again it was easy to make Daisy smile.

Lady Tremaine sipped her coffee, wondering when her little hellions would come storming into the front parlor. She loved her daughters, but they were quite the handful, and the older they got the more difficult it became to rein them in. She had been indulgent with her daughters after their father died. Giving them whatever they pleased, doting on them, finding them the best governess, taking them on splendid holidays, buying them whatever they wished. If they wanted new dresses, they got them. If they asked for horses to ride when they were in the country, Lady Tremaine could hardly say no. There was nothing her girls wanted that they didn't have, but this was the very reason they were becoming harder to please. Lady Tremaine dreamed of the day her daughters would be married. She dreamed of a life of her own with a man she loved. And if she was not lucky enough to find true love twice, she would be content with solitude.

But the quiet of the morning was disrupted the moment she contemplated her delightful future, as if her daughters sensed she was at ease and peace. Avery came in first as was his custom. "My lady, Nanny Pinch is here with Miss Anastasia and Miss Drizella."

Lady Tremaine winced. She couldn't help wishing she had waited just a few more precious moments before suggesting they should come see her. "Yes, show them in, Avery." She put down her coffee cup and motioned for it to be taken away.

Anastasia and Drizella were eleven and twelve, respectively. Neither of them looked like their mother, nor their father for that matter. The girls couldn't have been more different from their stately mother. While Lady Tremaine was angular and severe looking, she was still a very handsome woman. Her daughters were all points and edges. All legs and arms, with gawky necks, birdlike faces, and bulging eyes. They would have made remarkable witches, those two. But that is another story, a story that never happened, though it would be very intriguing to explore. Nevertheless, Lady Tremaine thought her daughters were beautiful and told them so at every opportunity.

On this day both girls were dressed in their fanciest day dresses, Anastasia in pale pink and Drizella in soft blue. They were ready for a day of shopping with Nanny Pinch. This would give Lady Tremaine the solitude she needed to prepare for their trip to the country, and Lady Tremaine was grateful to Nanny Pinch for having the foresight to get her girls out of the house for a few hours while she took care of the necessary arrangements.

Lady Tremaine adored Nanny Pinch. She was a sensible woman, still young and full of energy, which she needed in abundance to keep up with Anastasia and Drizella. She was a petite woman with dark hair and eyes and a splash of prominent freckles across her cute little nose and cheeks. She was hardly taller than the girls. Lady Tremaine laughed at the thought of her girls one day towering over their nanny.

"Good morning, my lovelies!" she said, smiling at her daughters.

Drizella always had the privilege of kissing her mother first, since she was the eldest. "Good morning, Mother," she said rather formally, making the lady laugh to herself. Lady Tremaine wondered how long they had practiced that in the schoolroom before they came downstairs. Anastasia, however, didn't stand on ceremony and leaped into her mother's arms.

"Good morning, Mama!" she said, almost knocking over the little round table with the coffee service.

"We discussed this, Anastasia," said Nanny Pinch, giving the girl a stern look. "If you refuse to act like a proper young lady, perhaps then it is best you stay in the nursery when we visit the country."

Zella's eyes grew larger than normal, and she pinched Anastasia hard on her upper arm.

"Ouch! Mama! Look what Zella did!"

Nanny Pinch quickly separated the girls. "Miss Anastasia, you sit there!" she said, pointing to one chair. "And, Miss Drizella, there!" she snapped, pointing to another. The chairs were on either side of a small table and situated across from Lady Tremaine, who was still residing on the velvet couch.

"Your mama doesn't have time for this nonsense! And it's not too late to change our plans for the country. We could just as easily stay here at home while your mama goes off and enjoys some much-needed time on her own." The girls clasped their hands together tightly and placed them on their laps, smiling sweetly. Lady Tremaine could see they were both doing their best impressions of proper young ladies, and she had to keep herself from laughing.

"That won't be necessary, Nanny Pinch. But we shall keep that option in reserve should my dear girls decide that a holiday in the country is just too much for them." Both of the girls wiggled in their seats, wanting desperately to squeal out but managing to keep their composure. Lady Tremaine smiled indulgently at her girls. "Don't you two look beautiful today. Miss Pinch tells me she is taking you out for a day of shopping. New dresses for our trip! I want you both looking your best and on your best behavior while we're in the country, do you understand?"

Both girls nodded their heads.

"Lady Hackle and her sons, Dicky and Shrimpy, will be there," said Lady Tremaine.

Drizella's eyes grew large again, making Anastasia laugh.

"Drizella has a crush on Dicky," she said, laughing harder. "She's going to make a fool of herself, Mama!"

Drizella practically leaped across the small table to slap her sister on the arm, knocking over a small jade dragon figurine in the process.

"Girls! Stop this at once! No one has a crush on anyone. And if you can't stop acting like little monsters, then you will stay at home!" said Lady Tremaine, starting to lose patience with them.

Drizella put her hands in her lap again. "Why shouldn't I have a crush on the young man Mama eventually wants me to marry?"

Though her daughter was right (Lady Tremaine and Lady Hackle did have plans for Stasia to marry Shrimpy and for Zella to marry Dicky), she felt Zella was far too young to be daydreaming about marriage.

"Well, I'm not going to marry anyone named Shrimpy!" Stasia wrinkled her nose, making her sister scoff.

"No one would want to marry you anyway!" cried Zella.

"Why would you want to marry someone named Dicky? That's a stupid name, too!" Stasia taunted.

"Hush now, both of you." Nanny Pinch was stern but calm. "Anastasia, you know perfectly well their names are Richard and Charles."

Stasia laughed again. "Well, Shrimpy seems like a silly nickname for someone named Charles. It doesn't make sense, and he's actually rather quite tall, so how he ended up with such a name is beyond me!"

"Once again you lack the wit to get the joke," Zella scoffed. "His name is Shrimpy *because* he is very tall. It's like calling a portly man Slim, or calling you Belle!" she added with a wicked grin.

"Oh, you!" said Stasia, leaping out of her seat and pulling the bows out of her sister's ringlets.

"That is enough! Both of you, stop this at once!" This time it wasn't Nanny Pinch who intervened, it was Lady Tremaine. Neither of the girls had ever heard their mother raise her voice to them, and it caused them both to stop their antics at once and stare at her. "I think Nanny Pinch is right. I have decided it's best if the two of you stay at home. How can I expect you to accompany me to the country if you can't behave like ladies?"

Both of the girls burst into tears, wailing and pleading with their mother to let them go. "I'm sorry, girls, I have been far too indulgent with you, and it is time for you to grow up. It's my fault really; I've spoiled you, but it's time you learn that there are consequences to your actions." Lady Tremaine thought she was doing what was best for her girls, who were far too used to getting their way. It was time she did something about it.

"Mother, please! Don't leave us alone with Nanny Pinch! Please. We won't see you for ages!" screamed Anastasia.

But Lady Tremaine was resolute. "No, my dear. I've made up my mind. I will be going on this trip without you. You will be in good hands with Nanny Pinch. Now, if you'll excuse me, I have a trip to prepare for. I suggest you go up to the classroom and finish your studies," said Lady Tremaine, trying her best to fool her girls into thinking she really intended to leave without them. The fact was, she was just trying to scare them into behaving.

"The classroom? But, Mother, what of our shopping trip? What about our new dresses?" screeched Drizella. Both of the girls were panicked.

"I can't believe you're doing this to us, Mama! I hate you!" said Anastasia, screwing up her face.

Lady Tremaine wasn't used to taking this sort of line with her daughters, and she didn't find it easy. In fact, she found it exhausting. It was causing her head to hurt, but she made her face passive and remote, and held her ground.

"I see no reason to buy you new dresses for a trip you will not be taking. And considering you hate me, I see no reason to bring you along."

Drizella dashed out of her seat and grabbed her mother's hands, pleading with her. "You really mean to leave us at home, Mama? This isn't a trick? I can't believe you would do this to us, your only daughters. The only things you have left of Papa. How do you think he would feel if he knew you were treating us so poorly? What would he think of you ruining my chances with the young Lord Hackle?"

Lady Tremaine took a deep breath and let it out with a heavy sigh. "I have ruined you. I gave you everything and this is how you treat me? You try to manipulate me by using the memory of your dear sweet father? You were so young when he died, you hardly knew him! He would find your behavior appalling. And he would be disappointed in me for raising you to become such terrible little beasts! I wanted this house to be a place of love, a place where people could show their emotions. I thought if I took a more active role in your lives you would love and respect me. That you wouldn't grow up resenting me, but I find now that I resent you! I should have just let you be raised by the servants. I should have limited my time to an hour a day after teatime like all the other ladies I know." She hated taking such a hard line with them, but she felt it was for their own good. "You're right, Zella, I was trying to trick you, to scare you into thinking I wasn't going to take you on this trip. I would have never dreamed of going anywhere without my precious girls, but at the moment I can't stand the sight of you! Nanny Pinch, take them upstairs at once, and that is where they will stay. Do you understand?"

Drizella and Anastasia cried and reached out for their mother as Nanny Pinch took them both by the arms and tried to lead them out of the room. It broke Lady Tremaine's heart to do this to her daughters, but she was at a loss. She had done it all wrong, and she worried she had ruined her daughters forever. She took another deep breath, pressed her fingers to her aching head, composed her emotions, and tried to sound stern.

"I will come up to say goodbye before I leave, girls. And, Nanny Pinch, please have Daisy sit with them. I want you to come back down so we can talk alone. Things are going to be very different around here from now on, and we have a lot to discuss before I leave for my trip."

Lady Tremaine watched as Nanny Pinch silently took her daughters out of the room. As soon as the door closed behind them she broke down in tears.

She had never been so harsh with her daughters before, but she didn't know what else to do. They had become unruly. Nanny Pinch had tried to discuss it with her in the past, but she had refused to see her daughters clearly. She had refused to believe they weren't the angels she had always seen them as. And she had to wonder what her husband would think of her now. He wouldn't have approved of the way she was raising their daughters, and he certainly wouldn't have approved of the casual manner in which she spoke with the servants. She had let things slip after he died.

Though he loved her and was always kind to her throughout their marriage, he had been a rigid man, always doing everything by the book, always proper and stoic, always on point. She loved him for it, and she didn't understand why she had changed so much after he died. Why she allowed herself to become so soft, so familiar with the servants.

As she sat there, she realized time away in the country without her daughters was exactly what she needed. She needed time to think. Time with her friends, riding horses and hunting foxes, time to play silly games without having to worry if her daughters were going to embarrass her.

Time to become herself again.

CHAPTER III

THE DRESS

Time in the English countryside was exactly what was in order. Lady Tremaine loved visiting these old estates. She always knew what to expect. There was a schedule to these gatherings, a protocol; it was orderly, and everything was just so. It was a nice reprieve from her chaotic life in London.

Before she left London she spoke at length with Nanny Pinch. The conversation made her miss the earlier train, but she needed to make clear what was expected. "I need you to be stern with my girls, Nanny Pinch. I won't have any more of these insolent outbursts. You have my express permission to be as strict with them as you deem fit. I want to see a marked improvement in them by the time I come back." Nanny Pinch was all too happy to comply. She had broached the subject on more than one occasion that something must be done about the girls. Lady Tremaine just hoped it wasn't too late to turn her little hellions around.

When Lady Tremaine's carriage finally pulled up in front of Lady Hackle's estate, her friend was there to greet her. She was so happy to have finally arrived after traveling all day by train. The carriage ride from the station wasn't terribly long, but it felt like an eternity after the long train journey, and she couldn't wait to be shown to her room so she could refresh herself after her long journey. Lady Hackle's estate was a lovely, grand, and stately place, adorned with gargoyles and stained glass. It was the sort of home you'd expect to be rife with suits of armor, though that wasn't Lady Hackle's style.

The footman quickly and quietly spirited Lady Tremaine's trunks away, closely supervised and followed by her lady's maid, Mrs. Bramble. Lady Tremaine had inherited Mrs. Bramble from her mother. She was an older woman, as prickly as her name suggested, and always ready to share gossip about what was going on downstairs. Her hair was entirely silver and wild. She didn't usually bother to keep it up in a bun, which was the fashion then, but she had made sure to tidy it up for their visit to the country. Lady Tremaine wondered what delicious tales she would hear from the servants on this trip.

"Good afternoon, my sweet friend," said Lady Hackle, holding out her arms in welcome.

"Good afternoon, Prudence," said Lady Tremaine, taking her hands and kissing her on the cheek. The ladies had been friends for many years and had become almost like sisters. Lady Tremaine always looked forward to their visits. Lady Hackle was a handsome woman, with light hair and eyes and an upturned button nose that Lady Tremaine found endearing. Something about her face had always reminded her of a sweet little rabbit.

Lady Hackle kept her gaze on the carriage, expecting to see Anastasia and Drizella step out next. "My dear, where are the girls? Are they coming in another carriage with Nanny Pinch?"

Lady Tremaine sighed. "I'm sorry, Prudence, neither of them are feeling well, and I thought it best they stay behind." Lady Tremaine didn't like lying to her old friend, but she didn't have the strength to tell her about the girls just yet. And what would she say, anyway? That she had spoiled them beyond redemption? That she feared she would be stuck with them into old age because they'd become so horrible no one would ever want to marry them? No. She wanted to rest and relax. This was her time, and honestly all she wanted to do was forget about her wretched little beasts, at least for the rest of the day.

Lady Hackle sighed. "Well, that is too bad about the girls. My boys will be devastated of course, but I suppose it can't be helped. Come in, my dear friend. I'm sure Pratt has already shown Mrs. Bramble to your rooms, and I imagine you are eager to refresh yourself after your long journey."

They walked into the great, imposing vestibule. It was done in the Roman style, a large, open room with marble pillars and magnificent statues of gods and goddesses scattered throughout. In the center of the room was an enormous staircase that split into two, leading to different wings of the house. A sweet-looking maid met them at the foot of the stairs.

"Dilly, please show Lady Tremaine to her room, though I dare say she already knows the way," said Lady Hackle with a warm smile. And then she added, "Oh yes, and, just a reminder, the dressing gong will be at six, dinner gong at eight. See you then." She left Lady Tremaine in Dilly's capable hands.

Lady Tremaine loved being on a schedule again. She and her husband had done everything on a schedule when he was alive. But she couldn't remember the last time Avery rang the dinner gong, let alone the dressing gong. She and the girls never dressed for dinner, not since Lord Tremaine died. She hadn't seen the reason for it. But now she understood why her husband had liked everything just so.

She realized she needed to be more of an example to her girls, and she planned to bring back her old ways of living the moment she returned.

When she got to her room—the Fairy Room, as Lady Hackle called it—she found Mrs. Bramble already unpacking and putting away her things. Lady Tremaine loved this room and typically stayed in it when she visited. She always felt like she was visiting a fairy's garden, with its purple-and-gold furnishings and delicate floral wallpaper.

"Everything is almost unpacked and put away, my lady." Mrs. Bramble had what Lady Tremaine thought of as a graveyard voice: quiet, serious, and almost foreboding.

"I see that, Mrs. Bramble. Thank you," Lady Tremaine said, looking around the room. Mrs. Bramble had thoughtfully laid out her gown for the evening, and somehow managed to find the time to have one of the maids start her a bath.

Both of their eyes darted toward the door when they heard someone knocking. Mrs. Bramble rushed to the door, opening it just a crack. "Oh hello,

Lady Hackle, please come in," she said, opening the door wider.

"Sorry for the intrusion, my dear Lady Tremaine. But I wanted to see what you will be wearing this evening. You've been in black far too long." She glanced at the dress on the bed, which was, unsurprisingly, black. Lady Hackle was being playful, of course, but she was right. Lady Tremaine had been wearing black since her husband had died, and though it had been quite some time since his passing, she couldn't bring herself to progress to wearing purple.

"Friend, it's been six years. I know you loved Francis—we all did, and we miss him dearly—but it's time to start living your life again. I shouldn't tell you this, but some of our old friends are starting to refer to you as the queen, as in Queen Victoria."

Lady Tremaine was taken aback. "Who is calling me that?" But she had to admit her friend was right, and she had to agree her clothing was rather stodgy and matronly. Perhaps it was time to lighten up. "I suppose you have an alternate dress in mind?" she asked with a knowing smile.

"Well, as a matter of fact I do!" It had been years since Lady Tremaine saw such a mischievous smile on Lady Hackle's face, not since they were girls together. She suddenly missed those days when she and Prudence were in school, not a care in the world other than making their mothers happy by finding the right husband, which they both did, to both of their mothers' satisfaction. Their mothers couldn't have been happier with their choices. The only thing that could have made them any more pleased was if they had come home with princes.

Lord Francis Tremaine was a mother's dream. He was a man of property and wealth, and came from one of the oldest and very best families. So did Prudence's husband, whom everyone called Piggy. Lady Tremaine laughed to herself, almost forgetting his actual name: Henry. She always found it amusing how most of the gentlemen in her circle had such ridiculous nicknames. Some of the ladies did as well, though thank goodness she never managed to acquire one. She couldn't imagine being called Bunny, or one of the other names fancied in her social circles. And now she was starting to fear everyone might take to calling her Vicky, since they've been calling her "the queen" behind her back.

She realized she had completely drifted out of the conversation she was having with Lady Hackle, and now her lady's maid had taken over the dress selections. While Lady Tremaine was musing, her friend had brought in a battalion of maids, each carrying a different dress, all of which Mrs. Bramble dismissed in succession.

"Come now, there has to be at least one you think will do," said Lady Hackle. "My dear Lady Tremaine, please, come over here and lend us your opinion. You will be wearing the dress, after all."

All the dresses were lovely, of course, exquisitely made in the latest fashions, but Lady Tremaine wasn't sure if they were right for her. It was clear Mrs. Bramble didn't think so, either.

"How about the dusty periwinkle with the deep

purple accents?" Lady Hackle motioned for one of the maids to hold it up so Lady Tremaine could see. "And maybe we can have my Rebecca do your hair this evening, just this once? Oh, you'll love her, my dear. I don't think Mrs. Bramble would mind, would you, Mrs. Bramble?"

Lady Tremaine laughed silently to herself, knowing full well Mrs. Bramble would mind. She would mind very much.

"That is up to my lady," Mrs. Bramble said stiffly.

But before Lady Tremaine could answer, her old friend seized the moment. "Delightful! I will send Rebecca in at six, then, to help with your hair. Oh, my sweet friend, you're going to look lovely tonight." She kissed Lady Tremaine on the cheek before dashing out of the room, her maids following her like a line of little ducklings.

Lady Tremaine sat on the bed as if exhausted. "Goodness, she is a whirlwind, isn't she?" she said, trying to make light of the situation, hoping Mrs. Bramble wouldn't be hurt or cross with her.

Mrs. Bramble simply stood there looking as if she had something to say but had decided to keep it to herself. "Go on, then," said Lady Tremaine. "I suppose you're upset with me. You know how Lady Prudence can be. She's tenacious when there is something she wants. Why not just give her this? And what would it hurt to wear purple? It's still a mourning color."

Mrs. Bramble took the black dress that she had previously laid out on the bed and hung it in the closet, saying nothing.

"Come now. Mrs. Bramble, don't be upset. You know how much I value you. I'm only letting Rebecca do my hair to make Lady Prudence happy." Still Mrs. Bramble said nothing. She just went about the room moving things a fraction of an inch from where they were before, pretending she was busy. "Mrs. Bramble, I must insist you speak your mind!" said Lady Tremaine, starting to become impatient.

Mrs. Bramble took the dress Lady Hackle had left and hung it on the outside of the wardrobe. "You realize what she's up to, don't you? There is a gentleman here she wants you to meet. It's all the talk downstairs. This entire party was planned so she could match the two of you, and I have to say, my lady, I don't approve." Mrs. Bramble took these liberties in the way she spoke to Lady Tremaine because she had worked for the family since Lady Tremaine was a little girl. But Lady Tremaine wondered how Mrs. Bramble would react to her new plan to run a tighter ship. She knew Avery would be on board—he was a by-the-numbers sort of man—but how would Mrs. Bramble handle it?

Lady Tremaine realized Mrs. Bramble had continued talking while she drifted off into her own thoughts. She was still going on about this mysterious man Lady Hackle wanted her to meet.

"No one has heard of him. He's not from these parts. They say he's royalty from some distant land who is looking for a new wife."

Lady Tremaine was intrigued but didn't let Mrs. Bramble know. "And what happened to his old wife, then?" she asked, trying to make light of the serious atmosphere in the room.

"Well, she died, of course." Mrs. Bramble scoffed. "There are wild stories about the land where he's from. They call it the Many Kingdoms. Oh, you should hear the tales, my lady! Mothers there often die mysteriously and well before their time, and these widowers always replace them with new wives who themselves meet a terrible fate." Mrs. Bramble's eyes were wide and her lips pursed. Lady Tremaine couldn't tell if Mrs. Bramble was angry or worried. Her eyes were full of concern, but her lips looked as if she was on the warpath. Perhaps she was both. "I won't have my lady bundled off to distant lands where stepmothers are reviled!"

Lady Tremaine knew what this was about. She had been her nanny, and then her mother's lady's maid, so she looked at Lady Tremaine almost like a daughter.

"Well, I don't intend to be bundled off anywhere, Mrs. Bramble, and as for these stories you've heard, must I remind you how foolish and bored some of these servants in the country can be? What else is there to do but weave hysterical tales about places they've never visited for themselves?"

Mrs. Bramble laughed. "I dare say they have their jobs to do," she said, but Lady Tremaine wondered. She imagined a bit of gossip downstairs was just the sort of thing the servants looked forward to.

"Well, I won't hear any more of this nonsense!" she said. She was becoming impatient and wanted to drop the subject, but Mrs. Bramble seemed to be bursting with more to say. "Oh, out with it then! I dare say you might explode if you don't share what's on your mind, Mrs. Bramble." She let a laugh escape, because it was all starting to sound ridiculous.

"This isn't a funny matter, my lady. You should hear the stories they tell downstairs: stepmothers being chased off cliffs and their souls being trapped in mirrors. One child's guardian was thrown from a tower, and another was slaughtered by the man who married her daughter! The Many Kingdoms is not a safe place."

Lady Tremaine wondered if the servants weren't

just winding up poor Mrs. Bramble. "Those sound like fairy stories to me, Mrs. Bramble. And when by the way did you have time to hear all these stories? You came directly here to unpack my things."

Mrs. Bramble took a book from her large carpetbag. "They aren't fairy stories, my lady. They are witch stories. True stories all recorded by foul witches who meddle in the lives of unsuspecting women." Mrs. Bramble looked desperate, and it became clear to Lady Tremaine something might be amiss with her lady's maid. She was, after all, quite old and would sometimes go on about odd things, but Lady Tremaine had never seen her get this worked up before.

"I see, Mrs. Bramble," she said, feeling a bit sad because she feared it might be time for Mrs. Bramble to retire. Of course, if it was best to replace Mrs. Bramble, Lady Tremaine would arrange a lovely cottage for her where she could live out her retirement, but she hadn't expected to have to make this decision during what was supposed to be her holiday away from household concerns.

"Here, my lady, take this and read it." Mrs. Bramble held up the book. "All the signs are there. You are just the sort of woman to fall into one of these stories. Beautiful, rich, sweet, and kind, tragically lost her husband too soon. But something will change; you will change. I don't know if it's the Many Kingdoms or the witches, but something causes the stepmothers in these stories to transform into horrible people. And it's not just the stepmothers; it's anyone these witches choose to meddle with."

Lady Tremaine sighed. "And what makes you think these witches will choose to meddle with me, my dear Mrs. Bramble? What do they know of me, living all the way in London so far away from these Many Kingdoms? What could these witches possible want with Lady Tremaine?"

Mrs. Bramble cackled, almost like she herself was a witch. "How am I to know the hearts and minds of witches? They're foul creatures, witches are, and I won't let my lady be dragged into their story!"

Lady Tremaine could see that Mrs. Bramble

was becoming even more agitated and was about to say something more, but she was tired of having this conversation and decided it was best if the old woman thought she believed her.

"Thank you, Mrs. Bramble. I will read the book, but I must insist you take the remainder of the evening to rest in your room. Do you understand? You're very worked up, and as much as I appreciate your devotion and care, I can't have you exhausting yourself."

Mrs. Bramble tried to protest. "But what of this evening, my lady? Who will help you dress?"

Lady Tremaine sighed. The old woman seemed to have forgotten about Rebecca.

"I suppose Rebecca will help me, just for this one evening, while you take a much-needed break. We might arrange a little holiday for you once we get back to London. Doesn't that sound nice? Is there anyone you'd like to visit? You haven't seen your sister in a while."

Mrs. Bramble was still clutching the book, squeezing it so tightly Lady Tremaine thought she might actually break her brittle fingers. "Here, let me take that from you, Mrs. Bramble. I promise to read it. Think about where you'd like to have your holiday, and I'll make all the arrangements." Lady Tremaine pulled the cord hanging near the fireplace mantel to summon a maid, who showed up within moments. Lady Tremaine loved how efficiently Lady Hackle ran her household.

"Hello, dear," Lady Tremaine said. "Could you please take Mrs. Bramble to her room and have someone bring her tea and later her dinner on a tray? She isn't feeling well."

"I don't want to be any trouble or make more work for the cook or other servants." Mrs. Bramble was fussing. "They have enough to do with the party this evening."

"Nonsense," said Lady Tremaine. "They won't mind, will they, dear?"

The maid smiled. "We won't mind at all," she said gently, being kind to the old woman. "Come now, Mrs. Bramble, let me show you to your room."

Seeing Mrs. Bramble walk out of the room with

the young maid made her look even older in Lady Tremaine's eyes. She hadn't realized how very old her lady's maid had become, and she suddenly felt rather foolish for not having seen it before.

"You rest, Mrs. Bramble. And I'll be very disappointed if I hear you haven't."

Mrs. Bramble gave her lady a weak smile. "Yes, my lady. Don't you worry about old Mrs. Bramble. I'll be right as rain again tomorrow. Just remember what I said."

Lady Tremaine smiled at the old woman. "I'll remember. Now go, and don't leave that bed until you are fully restored," she said as the women walked out of the room.

When she had gone, Lady Tremaine rang the bell to summon another maid, then sat on the bed with a sigh. She had come to the country to relax, not contend with antics such as these. She briefly wondered how Anastasia and Drizella were doing, but before she could get up to write them a quick letter, there was a knock at the door.

"Come in." This time it was a tall, lanky girl, all arms and legs. "Yes, could you please let Lady Hackle know I will need Rebecca to help me dress this evening? Thank you, dear."

The young maid nodded and skittered out of the room, awkwardly mumbling something as she left. Lady Tremaine shook her head. She realized the dressing gong had already sounded while she had been talking with Mrs. Bramble, and now it looked like she might be late.

Perhaps it's best I don't impress this gentleman from dangerous lands, she thought, laughing to herself.

Chapter IV

The Mysterious Sir Richard

Lady Tremaine needn't have worried about arriving late to dinner. Rebecca dressed her and did her hair with dexterous skill and speed, and she descended in time for dinner after all.

The guests gathered in a large, beautiful room. Two crystal chandeliers holding white candles cast a lovely glow on everyone assembled, catching on jewelry and sequins and causing everything to glitter. Lady Tremaine always found the ladies in these circles amusing. To her they looked like vibrant, exotic birds decked out in all their finery, in contrast to the gentlemen in their black tails. Lady Tremaine preferred the way of actual birds, the male birds with their colorful plumage and the lady birds in their somber browns and blacks.

She had gotten used to mourning-period clothes. She hadn't been able to bring herself to progress to purple until this evening, and that was only to make her friend happy. So tonight she, too, felt like one of the lady birds, glittering and showy, and she wasn't sure how that made her feel. It suddenly seemed very audacious to be wearing purple. But she quickly reasoned it was the customary transition color between black and more vibrant colors after the mourning period, and Lady Hackle was probably right. It had been six years; it *was* time to move on.

Lady Tremaine didn't quite know what to do with herself. Some of the guests were milling around the room chatting with each other, while others were sitting in little groups on the velvet chairs and love seats having lively conversations. She didn't quite feel like herself in the dress her friend had picked out for her. She told herself she wasn't betraying her husband's memory by wearing it.

Though the mourning period was long over,

she still felt her clothing should reflect her loss and heartbreak. She tried to ignore the tiny twinge that told her she was ready to find love again, even though it shone within her like the sparkling gray crystals that decorated the bodice of her dress and the matching necklace, earrings, and bracelet Lady Hackle had lent her that evening.

Then a delightful feeling came over her: she suddenly realized it was precisely because she didn't feel like herself that she indeed felt beautiful that evening.

Rebecca had done a remarkable job on her hair, and it did look fetching with the dress Lady Hackle had picked out for her. She fancied the crystals on her dress lent a glint to the hints of silver in her hair. She wasn't a young woman, but she didn't feel she was old enough for her hair to be quite so streaked with silver. This evening, for some reason, she liked the way she looked. It made her feel stately, as if the silver was a badge of wisdom, and perhaps even of her heartbreak. It had only begun to show in the years since her husband had passed away.

She felt that she had acquired a lot of new things since her husband died. The most surprising, though it shouldn't have been, was that her little girls were now almost young women. They seemed to transform overnight, though it felt like only a few short months ago that they were just little things running around the house, tormenting their nanny or stealing treats from the cook and then hiding in the pantry to eat their plunder.

And then she remembered the evenings where she would sit with them until they fell asleep, crying themselves into exhaustion because they missed their father so much. Anastasia and Drizella had cried so many tears for their father, there had been no room for her own. Lady Tremaine had to be strong for her girls and do whatever she could to make them happy again. Her heart ached a little for those days. She wondered if it had been a good idea to leave them in London, but she knew if they were going to learn their lesson, it was the right thing to do, though she hoped keeping them at home hadn't decreased their chances of a match with Lady Hackle's boys.

As she looked around the room, she didn't see any faces she didn't recognize. It was the usual set of lords and ladies, and she had to wonder if this mysterious man Mrs. Bramble had been going on about actually existed. Perhaps it was all just downstairs talk. If there was indeed any talk downstairs at all.

And then she saw him. He looked completely out of place. Not because he wasn't a gentleman or finely dressed, but because he was *too* good looking. He had dark hair and striking eyes, and there was something about him that set him apart from the other men in the room.

They didn't make men like him in London. He was too perfect, with his finely sculpted features, his strong jaw and cleft chin. He was like something out of a fairy tale. She wouldn't be surprised if his name were Prince Dashing, that's how perfect he was. She had never seen such a handsome man possessing such an unmistakable boyish charm. She could see it from across the room as he talked to

Lady Hackle, the two of them laughing, her friend completely charmed by him.

She could almost swear they were talking about her. She wondered if she was blushing, then scolded herself for acting like a giddy schoolgirl. She quickly sorted out her fluttering feelings, set herself straight, and choked down her nervousness. She had never felt in less control of her feelings before, but she managed to gather herself just in time for Lady Hackle and this mysterious man to make their way across the room to where she was standing.

"Lady Tremaine," Lady Hackle said, "I would like to introduce you to Sir Richard. He is visiting us from the Many Kingdoms."

Lady Tremaine smiled and put out her hand. "So this is the much-talked-about Sir Richard. It is lovely to meet you," she said as the gentleman kissed her hand.

"I'm honored to meet you, Lady Tremaine." He looked her in the eye with such intensity that her heart started to flutter again.

"So, tell me about these Many Kingdoms, Sir

Richard. I find it interesting that so many kingdoms could coexist without conflict. That so many kings and queens could reside in such close proximity peacefully."

Sir Richard laughed. "Oh, the courts within the Many Kingdoms have their local conflicts but never with neighboring kingdoms. There always seems to be some wicked person causing trouble for one kingdom or another, but never in ours. Thankfully in our corner of the Many Kingdoms we are a peaceful court free of wickedness. I wish I could say the same for our neighboring kingdom; it is rumored there is a beast there that runs wild."

A beast! Well, that was certainly unusual and mysterious. Lady Tremaine wanted to keep the conversation going, and she knew the best way was to ask questions. She was suddenly happy her mother had sent her away to finishing school as a girl, as she was quite adept at the art of being a lady. To that end, while she was curious to hear more about this beast, she didn't want Sir Richard to think she was too interested in the more unusual aspects of his homeland. "And what sorts of local conflicts are there, Sir Richard?"

It felt odd calling this man by his first name, too intimate for someone she had just met, but she was already besotted with him.

"Oh the usual sort of thing," he said, smiling. "There was the old queen who tried to have her daughter killed because she was jealous of her beauty. You know, the typical problems you might find in any kingdom." He said this so offhandedly that Lady Tremaine laughed.

"I'd hardly call that usual. It sounds like fairy tales," she said.

"Well, nothing of the sort has ever happened in my hamlet's court," said Sir Richard. "It's a peaceful place. So far, our kingdom has been left out of the book of fairy tales, and we intend to keep it that way."

Lady Tremaine thought that was an odd thing to say. "So this book of fairy tales is real, then? I've heard talk of it." She did not want to mention her servant's hysterics, nor the fact that she now wondered if the book he was referring to was in fact the very same book Mrs. Bramble had just given her.

Sir Richard laughed. "Oh, it's real, but greatly exaggerated, I assure you. For example, I have never seen these witches who are said to author this book. I think they're pure fiction."

Lady Tremaine smiled. "Then I imagine this is the Many Kingdoms' version of a history book. Ours, too, are greatly exaggerated, I imagine," she said.

Lady Hackle cleared her throat. "Now, now, Lady Tremaine, don't let the gentleman hear you say such things."

Sir Richard laughed. Just then the dinner gong sounded, and all the assembled ladies and gentlemen began to pair off and line up to go into the dining room.

"Sir Richard, would you mind escorting Lady Tremaine into the dining room, as you are both without partners this evening?" asked Lady Hackle with a wide smile.

"It would be my greatest pleasure," he said, taking Lady Tremaine's arm. To Lady Tremaine's surprise she and Sir Richard were among the first to go in after Lord and Lady Hackle, which was slightly confusing, but she surmised that his title might have held more prestige in his own lands than it did in hers.

Lady Hackle had arranged a magnificent feast. Lady Tremaine always thought she was an exceptional hostess, but tonight she could hardly eat a thing. She was enraptured by Sir Richard, who was becoming more interesting to her by the moment. She hardly thought of her girls that evening at dinner, not until Sir Richard asked about them.

"Lady Prudence tells me you have two lovely daughters," he said.

"Yes, Anastasia and Drizella. They have been my world since Lord Tremaine passed away." She didn't see the point in mentioning it was probably the reason they had become snotty little twits spoiled past redemption and that she'd had to leave them home.

"I also have a daughter," he said. "Aren't they our greatest treasures?" He was looking at her intently.

Lady Tremaine kept her face passive, not wanting to scare the man off with tales about her wicked girls. She wondered if it was too late for her daughters, hoping she hadn't ruined any chance of them becoming the young ladies she and Lord Tremaine hoped they would become.

To hear Sir Richard talk about his angelic daughter, one would think she was a treasure, fashioned by the gods out of all that was good and glittering and bestowed to him from the heavens. He must have raised her well. Lady Tremaine was envious really, thinking of how awful both her daughters had been to her before she left for this trip, and she probably only knew the half of their usual misdeeds. She decided she'd better sit down and chat with Nanny Pinch when she returned to see how deeply this behavior had taken hold of them. She felt more than ever that she had done everything wrong after her husband died.

As she sat next to this enchanting gentleman, she realized she had lost something of herself over the past six years. She had lost her edge, her wit, and her stoicism. She had become soft, and she resolved to find herself again.

Chapter V

The Gift

Lady Tremaine woke the next morning to Rebecca opening the curtains in the Fairy Room. She hated to admit it, but it was a nice change to have Rebecca looking after her. She was a happy young woman, with ginger hair, green eyes, and a willowy stature, almost fairylike.

"Good morning, my lady. I have brought you some coffee," said Rebecca as she tied back the long purple curtains.

"Thank you, Rebecca dear. What does Lady Hackle have planned for us today?"

Rebecca walked over to the bed and began arranging the pillows so that Lady Tremaine could enjoy her coffee sitting up. "The gentlemen are in the vestibule enjoying some libations before heading out for their hunt," she said.

Lady Tremaine thought she would like to be there now to see Sir Richard off. She imagined he looked dashing in his hunting clothes. "And the ladies? What will the ladies be doing today?" she asked as Rebecca placed the coffee tray on the bed.

"The gentlemen will be joining the ladies for a picnic this afternoon after their hunt," said Rebecca.

Lady Tremaine thought that sounded lovely. "And how is Mrs. Bramble?" she asked, taking a sip of her coffee. "Have you seen her this morning, Rebecca?"

"Yes, that's how I knew you wished for nothing but coffee this morning," the young maid said, smiling. "She seems to be feeling much better and is quite eager to attend her lady. But I'm not sure she's ready to return to her duties."

Lady Tremaine wondered if she shouldn't just send Mrs. Bramble back home. "Tell her it is my wish that she continue to rest—that is, if Lady Prudence can spare you. I wouldn't like to deprive her of her lady's maid."

Rebecca looked pleased. "Lady Prudence is being well taken care of. I am entirely at your service. Unless you'd prefer Mrs. Bramble?" she said, taking Lady Tremaine's dressing gown out of the wardrobe.

The fact was, she didn't prefer Mrs. Bramble. Lady Tremaine was enjoying this change of pace, without her daughters and the servants who knew her well. She felt it was a chance to start fresh, to regain her old self. There was an ease to being cared for by Rebecca and the rest of Lady Hackle's servants. It was all entirely civil, without the overfamiliarity she had fallen into at home. She liked feeling that everyone knew their place, and with that she realized that she, too, had found hers.

"No, Rebecca, Mrs. Bramble should rest a while longer. I think she is well where she is. Now let's decide what I will wear to the picnic. I assume my dear friend Lady Prudence has some ideas on the matter?" she asked teasingly.

"As a matter of fact, she did give me a few dresses for you to choose from. Shall I show them to you now?" Rebecca held out a long black silk robe with vivid pink flowers for Lady Tremaine to wear while she made her selections for the day. "I asked one of the maids to come up and run a bath for you. Why don't we take a look at the dresses while we wait?"

Just then a dainty young woman in a black-and-white maid's uniform came into the room.

"Rose, please run a bath for Lady Tremaine. We will be in shortly," Rebecca said.

The slight girl nodded and quickly went into the adjoining bathroom without another word.

"Don't mind Rose, my lady, she is very shy," Rebecca continued. "I think all the dresses Lady Prudence picked out for you are exquisite, but I have a feeling you will like this one best." She held up a periwinkle-and-white day dress. "And look at this," she added, excited as a young schoolgirl as she pointed to the matching hat and gloves.

"Oh yes, that is beautiful. And such a beautiful shade." Lady Tremaine traced the tips of her fingers over the fabric. The dress was a delicate shade of periwinkle, trimmed with white lace along the neckline, sleeves, and hem. The hat was white with periwinkle flowers.

"I thought you'd like this one best," Rebecca said as Rose came out of the bathroom.

"The lady's bath is ready," said Rose.

"Thank you, Rose. Please hang this up while I attend Lady Tremaine." Rebecca handed her the dress, then turned her attention back to the lady.

"My lady, I almost forgot. Mrs. Bramble asked me to keep this safe for you, but not to give it to you. She said something about a witch's curse, or maybe it was a pirate's, I'm not sure. Either way, I thought it was best that you should have it. I didn't feel right keeping it from you." She held out a small satin box.

Lady Tremaine took the box from Rebecca's

hand knowing exactly what was inside. "Poor Mrs. Bramble. Was she really talking of curses? I feel just awful bringing her on this trip without realizing she wasn't up to it," said Lady Tremaine. She was terribly worried about her lady's maid.

"Don't worry, my lady. Her behavior is a bit concerning, but she is in good hands downstairs. I promise you," said Rebecca.

"Thank you, Rebecca, I don't know what I would do without you," she said as she opened the box to reveal an oval green brooch in its antique gold setting. Her heart sank looking at the brooch her husband had given her. They had chosen it together in a little shop near Eaton Square. They had been taking a stroll in the park when her husband suggested an alternate path home and they came upon the funny little shop. It wasn't the sort of place her husband would usually frequent, but he seemed to have a purpose in taking her there, like he had planned it from the beginning. She remembered it vividly as if it had just happened the other day and not over six years ago now.

"Did you plan this, dear? Have you been here before?" she had asked as they reached the shop doors.

"No, my dear, I've never seen this shop before, but let's go inside," he'd said with a cheeky look that was out of character for him. She thought he was playing with her, and she decided to go along with his little ruse, because she was sure he had some sort of surprise in mind.

When they walked into the shop, a brass bell rang overhead. It was a dim little place with a long glass case displaying the treasures within. She remembered her husband going right over to the case, not even noticing the proprietor had come out from behind a curtain. He was a happy sort of man, beaming with excitement to have customers, even if it seemed they had just interrupted his lunch. He was still holding his napkin, wiping his hands with it as he approached the display case.

"So sorry to come at your lunchtime," said Lady Tremaine, smiling at the shopkeeper. "I am Lady Tremaine, and this is my husband, Lord Tremaine."

"Welcome, my lady. We don't get many lords

and ladies in my little shop. It's an honor. Are you looking for anything in particular?" he asked.

Just then her husband looked up from the case. "Good man, I'd like to see this brooch here!"

The shopkeeper rushed over to the case and took the tray with the brooch along with a number of other exquisite pieces. "My love, come here. Look at this brooch. What do you think?"

Lady Tremaine went over to the case. The brooch caught her eye immediately. "It's a lovely brooch, my dear."

Her husband looked up at her, meeting her eyes. "And it will look so handsome on you, my love. It's beautiful and stately just like you."

Lady Tremaine hadn't seen her husband so excited in quite some time. He had been so tired and not himself that she had started to worry about his health, and she was cheered to see him in such fine spirits.

She took the brooch in her hands, almost mesmerized by its beauty and how it made her feel. She felt a tingling sensation move through her, which made her feel exhilarated, and powerful, and yet at the same time somehow very calm.

"And it has an interesting story," said the shopkeeper. "I bought everything on this tray from a dealer who says he purchased the entire lot from a pirate, along with a book of fairy tales that is said to be written by witches."

Lord Tremaine scoffed. "Poppycock!" he said, scandalizing his wife.

"What my husband meant to say was surely that's just a story you tell to entice your customers, isn't that right, darling?" asked Lady Tremaine.

Before her husband could answer, a little boy came bounding into the room. He was a bold creature, dark-haired with eyes that one could describe as sad for how large they were, but this child was a jolly little fellow, and quite brave.

"My father doesn't tell lies, my lady! The dealer saw the pirate himself! He said the pirate wore a funny hat, and even sold him those gold boot buckles on that tray! And you wouldn't believe what else he had—"

The shopkeeper stepped in.

"That's enough, son. Go back upstairs. The lord and lady don't have time to hear about pirates," he said as he watched his son go through the curtain and upstairs in a huff, looking back every few steps to see if they would call him to rejoin the conversation.

"I'm sorry about that. He gets very excited. I'm happy he takes an interest, because one day this business will be his, and one day his son's. It will be my legacy."

Lord Tremaine sighed. "It's a fine thing to have a son to leave your legacy to, and what a brave young lad he is to stand up for his father that way." Then he laughed, adding, "Well, if you both say the dealer bought these items from a pirate, who am I to say he didn't." He saw Lady Tremaine was running her fingers across the brooch. "My darling, you do like the brooch, don't you?" he asked.

She couldn't help but feel that he had brought her here specifically to get this brooch. "I do like it, my husband," she said, taking it in her hands. "I love it, in fact."

Lord Tremaine clapped his hands together, laughing. "Ah! See that! She likes it, my good man! Then we shall take it!"

Lady Tremaine had never seen him in such a jovial mood. It wasn't like him to act so gregariously in public, or to go into poky little shops for that matter. But it didn't matter; he seemed well again and that made her heart happy.

Lady Tremaine looked up from the brooch as the memory faded, and she found herself back in the Fairy Room at Lady Hackle's home. It was such a fond memory, going into that little shop with her husband, one of the last lovely days they'd had together. Soon after, she had lost her husband to the illness she thought he was recovering from on that outing. She found herself having to banish the images of him on his deathbed and choke down the memory of their last words to each other, trying to root herself instead in the present, doing her best to replace the sad images of her departed husband with lovely ones of a bright and beautiful future, perhaps even with Sir Richard.

The thought surprised her. She hadn't realized how much she wanted this man. Here she was imagining a future with him. A future where she and her daughters lived happily with Richard and his daughter.

"Are you well, my lady?" asked Rebecca.

"Yes, Rebecca, I was just lost in the past, and perhaps the future. I'm careful not to linger there too often for fear of being lost there forever and not seeing what is in front of me." She handed the brooch back to the lady's maid.

"Shall I put this out with your other jewelry, then? Would you like to wear it today to the picnic?" Rebecca asked.

"No, Rebecca, it doesn't go with my dress. But I'd like you to leave it on my vanity. Perhaps I will wear it this evening at dinner," she said, staring at it one last time before Rebecca closed the box.

"I'm sorry, my lady, but I have to ask: you're

not worried about Mrs. Bramble's ravings about the brooch being cursed, are you? It's all nonsense if you ask me," said Rebecca.

"Is that what you would call it, Rebecca? Ravings? Is it that bad with Mrs. Bramble?" she asked.

"I'm afraid so, my lady."

Lady Tremaine wanted to chalk it up to an old woman's wild imagination, but recalling her conversation with the shopkeeper gave her pause. "The funny thing is, Rebecca, I just remembered the shopkeeper telling Lord Tremaine and me that he had acquired it from a mysterious dealer along with a number of other items, including a book of fairy tales written by witches. I wonder if this is the same book Mrs. Bramble gave me. And I'm almost sure he mentioned some sort of curse, but it has been so long since that day. Maybe I'm mistaken."

Rebecca frowned. "Perhaps Mrs. Bramble is simply remembering the story you shared with her back then."

Lady Tremaine shook her head. "I can't believe I didn't think of that myself. Of course, that's what happened. And she's somehow managed to get it all jumbled in her head. Tell me, Rebecca, has there been talk downstairs about Sir Richard?"

Rebecca smirked. "No more than the usual when a handsome man comes to visit. The maids and some of the footmen are swooning, of course. I mean, he is a very good-looking man."

Lady Tremaine laughed. "And is there any talk about the Many Kingdoms, where Sir Richard is from? Mrs. Bramble would have me believe it is a dangerous place."

Rebecca looked uncomfortable.

"Out with it, Rebecca. What are they saying down there?"

Rebecca cleared her throat. "Well, my lady, if you don't mind my saying so, I think Mrs. Bramble is getting on in age and might be confused. I honestly haven't heard any disturbing stories about Sir Richard or the Many Kingdoms from anyone other than Mrs. Bramble herself." Rebecca looked as if she felt bad for saying so.

Everything was starting to make sense. "I see," said Lady Tremaine. She realized it was probably best that Mrs. Bramble had left the book of fairy tales with her and wasn't reading it obsessively.

"I hope I didn't speak out of turn, my lady," Rebecca said.

"No, Rebecca, you didn't. You said exactly what I needed to hear."

CHAPTER VI

THE UNDERSTANDING

Ladies Tremaine and Hackle were enjoying some time to themselves away from the other guests in Lady Hackle's parlor, which was so much grander than her own. With its French doors and its abundance of ferns and exotic flowers, it was almost like a solarium. She thought about how lovely it would be in the future for her and Lady Hackle to be old together, watching their grandchildren run around in this room. Lady Hackle often suggested that Lady Tremaine come live there once their children were married, and if she didn't like the idea of living in the big house with all of them, she could live in the dowager house if she preferred, since there was no dowager in residence. Lady Tremaine loved the idea and always held it in reserve should she never marry again.

She had a lovely afternoon with her dear old friend while the rest of the guests were taking their leisure in their rooms after the picnic. It was the perfect opportunity for the two ladies to sneak off and chat.

"Won't the other ladies feel like we've left them out?" asked Lady Tremaine, feeling a bit like a naughty schoolgirl and making Lady Hackle laugh.

"Well, we won't tell the other ladies. Most of them are sleeping anyway. The dressing gong won't be for ages, so we have all the time in the world to gossip! Don't get me wrong, I love these gatherings, but sometimes I need a little time to myself. Take it from me, there is nothing like a long afternoon outdoors to make your guests retire to their rooms," she said, laughing again.

"I want to hear all about your walk with Sir Richard." Lady Hackle's eyes were alight, giddy for her friend. "You two seemed so enchanted with each other at the picnic. I didn't dare come over and interrupt, and the next thing I knew the two of you were gone. I must have all the details."

Lady Tremaine remained silent, fidgeting with a spare thread on the hem of her sleeve, trying to avoid Lady Hackle's question. "Will you just look at that?" she said, showing her friend the thread on her sleeve. "I'd better bring it to Rebecca's attention."

Lady Hackle gave her friend a knowing look. "Come on, my dear, something is going on between the two of you, you can't deny it. And I want to know everything, now spill!" she said, laughing and prodding her friend.

"I don't deny it, Prudence, I just don't know where to begin. He's perfect. In every single possible way," said Lady Tremaine.

Lady Hackle looked very pleased with herself. "What did you talk about? What did he say?" Lady Hackle asked, leaning in as if Lady Tremaine were about to tell her a secret.

"We spent much of the time talking about his

home, how lovely it was and how lonely he's been since his wife passed away. He talked of wanting a mother for his daughter, someone to raise her, and to be a wife to him. He spoke of combining our wealth to create a secure future for our children, and for ourselves," she said, drifting off to their conversation, remembering how much she wanted him to kiss her. But he was far too much the gentleman to do so.

"Did he ask you to marry him?" her friend asked, clearly eager to see if she could commend herself on her matchmaking skills.

"Not yet. I think he wanted to see if I was disposed to the idea before proposing," said Lady Tremaine, still looking at the bit of thread on her sleeve.

She didn't want her friend to know how very much she liked this gentleman. She didn't really want to admit it to herself. It all seemed so sudden, so out of the blue, and she wondered if she was being foolish. But that's how things were done in these circles—you met someone, married them, and then found out after you were married if you were a good match. If you were, all the better, and if not, then you spent most of your time apart. Most marriages in Lady Tremaine's circle were about combining families, social capital, and resources. Too few were inspired by actual love. She had been fortunate with her first marriage. Not only did her family approve of the match, but they were a good couple. But she had somehow thought the second time she found love she would do things differently, take her time. And now she found herself dashing into another marriage without knowing much about the gentleman.

"What will you say if he asks you tonight? You have to say yes," said Lady Hackle, pink-cheeked as if it were she herself who was in love.

"We don't know each other that well, Prudence. Doesn't it all seem too quick?" asked Lady Tremaine.

"What is there to know? He's a rich man and lives in an enchanted kingdom. He's handsome, dashing, and highly ranked. He's a dream!" said Lady Hackle, taking her friend's hand.

"I'm not sure what I will say, Prudence. We didn't speak of love. Though I suppose the implication was there." Lady Tremaine looked up at her friend. She was surprised how much she wanted this man to love her. She feared she was treading into dangerous territory.

"Tell me everything. From beginning to end. Leave nothing out. Not a single word. And then we'll know what you should do," said Lady Hackle.

Lady Tremaine took a deep breath. "Very well, Prudence, if you insist. You know what a lovely day it was. You picked the perfect place for our picnic. It was such a gorgeous spot, everything was green, the flowers in bloom, and you know how fond I am of the gazebo across the lake. After the gentlemen returned from their hunt, Sir Richard made his way to me almost immediately and suggested we take a walk. We crossed the little wooden bridge over the lake, and there we talked until you sent Pratt over to let us know everyone was going back to the house. I spoke of my daughters, and he spoke of his, and we talked of what life had been like for both of us after our spouses died. He's such a practical man, very much like the men here in London. Everything was so sensible. We didn't speak of love, though he did speak of how he longed for a woman to run his household, to raise his daughter. He spoke of his loneliness, and how much he missed his wife, and how he'd like to have companionship again. And I understood him, because I want those things, too. But I couldn't help but wonder if he wanted love."

"Of course he does. He spoke of his loneliness and wanting a wife. What else could he have meant?" asked her friend.

"I feel that is what he meant. At least that is how it felt in the moment. But I might have been swept away by the beauty of it all," said Lady Tremaine.

"Oh, I've seen the way he looks at you. He has eyes for no one else when you're in the room. I think he is in love with you." Lady Hackle squeezed Lady Tremaine's hand.

Lady Tremaine thought Lady Hackle may be right. She felt the same way, and then she realized she knew what she would do.

"If he asks me, Prudence, I do think I will say yes," she said, taking her hand out of her friend's and putting it to her heart. "Can you believe it? Me, marrying again, and moving off to the Many Kingdoms? As if one king or queen wasn't enough, now I'll be living in a place where the lands are littered with royalty." Lady Tremaine giggled along with her friend. The giddiness was contagious.

"I imagine your life there with Sir Richard will be quite extravagant," said Lady Hackle. "Oh, you will have to invite me to visit once you are settled. I have to see your new château."

"He hasn't asked me to marry him yet, Prudence!" Lady Tremaine looked up at the sound of the dressing gong. Her heart skipped a beat at the thought of seeing Sir Richard again at dinner.

"Oh my, is it already time to get dressed?" said Lady Hackle. "I thought we had ages. We'd better go upstairs and get ready. I want you looking especially beautiful this evening."

Lady Tremaine laughed and shook her head at

her friend. She had to wonder if they were making too much of all this.

"By the way, how are you finding Rebecca? Are you happy with her?" asked Lady Hackle, rising from the table to make her way to her room to get ready.

"Oh, she's delightful. Thank you so much for letting her attend me while I've been here," said Lady Tremaine.

"Brilliant. Then you shall keep her. She told me of your troubles with poor old Mrs. Bramble, and she did mention how much she'd love to travel with you to the Many Kingdoms, so I suggested that if you were agreeable, she should stay with you." Lady Hackle smiled knowingly, and Lady Tremaine let out a loud laugh.

"Oh, you two have been plotting to get me married off, have you?" said Lady Tremaine.

"Well, my dear, I'd say it was about time, wouldn't you? And why not to a man who looks as if he's stepped out of the pages of a romance story!

I can see you two riding away on a white horse, and I hope you do! I'd love nothing more than to see you happy."

⚜ ⚜ ⚜ ⚜

Once back in her room, Lady Tremaine gave herself over to Rebecca entirely, letting her dictate her clothing and jewelry and style her hair as she chose. She usually wasn't one for fussing over her appearance, but she wanted to be especially stunning at dinner that evening.

"You look beautiful, my lady," Rebecca marveled. "I'm sure Sir Richard will find you captivating."

Lady Tremaine narrowed her eyes at the young woman. "Has there been talk downstairs, Rebecca? About Sir Richard and me?"

Rebecca blushed. "I admit there has, my lady. One of the upstairs maids says she overheard Sir Richard and his valet discussing plans to return to the Many Kingdoms tonight once dinner is over, but he wants to speak to you first."

Lady Tremaine flushed, even as a sense of dread went through her. Why was he leaving? And why must he speak with her? She had hoped they would have more time together, and she couldn't imagine it was his plan to ask her to marry him if he was leaving this evening. She suddenly felt rather foolish for decking herself out in red velvet and letting Rebecca adorn her hair in sparkling rubies to match.

It was the first time she hadn't worn mourning colors since her husband's death. She had even fastened the jade brooch her husband had given her right in the center of her bodice, making it the crowning piece of her gown. Before Rebecca had told her of Sir Richard's plans to leave, Lady Tremaine had felt like a new woman who respected and cherished her past but chose not to be lost in it, because she was very much looking forward to her future. But now she didn't know what to expect. She had been so excited and so looking forward to this new love affair, and now she felt foolish and adrift once more.

"Everything will be just fine, my lady, I'm sure if it," said Rebecca, helping Lady Tremaine with her long white gloves. "In fact I know it. I often get feelings about how things will turn out, and I think you and Sir Richard are destined for each other." She went to the door. "Are you ready to go down?" she asked, holding it open with a smile.

"Yes, Rebecca, I suppose I am as ready as I ever will be."

Lady Tremaine felt nervous milling around the drawing room, waiting for everyone to assemble for dinner. Sir Richard hadn't arrived yet, and she was starting to wonder if he had just gone straight back to the Many Kingdoms, deciding not to speak with her before leaving after all.

But then she saw him. He looked as if he had stepped out of the pages of Mrs. Bramble's book of fairy tales. He was far too dashing for his own good, and she felt her face flush again as she wondered what he wanted to discuss. She felt slightly dizzy as he made his way over to her, not even stopping to make polite conversations with those he passed. She was in his direct path, his eyes were fixed on her, and she couldn't help but feel like hunted prey. He had such a serious look on his face, which made her heart flutter, because she was sure he was about to disappoint her. Men often looked serious when they were about to disappoint a lady.

"My dear Lady Tremaine," he said as he approached, "may I speak with you in the garden before dinner starts?"

"I think we have time." She looked at the little gold clock on the mantel.

"Lady Hackle said we can take as much time as we need," he replied, and took her by the hand, leading her out the double doors into the garden.

They walked over to a pond that was filled with tiny sparkling lights. When she got closer, she saw that they were little mirrored bowls floating on the surface of the water, candles flickering within them, casting remarkable shards of light that danced across Sir Richard's face and the garden.

"You wanted to speak with me about something, Sir Richard?" she said, standing very still as she awaited his reply. She felt she had to brace herself for what he was about to say. She feared his words would be a blow and she wanted to be ready. She tried to make herself solid and unmovable. Ready for impact.

"I did. I'm afraid I have to leave right after dinner, but I didn't feel it would be right to leave without speaking to you first, not after our talk earlier today. I wanted to make sure there was no misunderstanding. I wouldn't want to leave if there was indeed more we had to say."

Lady Tremaine's heart sank. This was what she had feared and expected. Of course their conversation had not been the start of a passionate love affair or a new adventure. It had been nothing more than polite small talk.

"You needn't say more, Sir Richard. I understand you completely," she said. She felt foolish for thinking their talk today was anything more than two people who had lost their spouses, connecting over their shared pain. She thought he had spoken of wanting a wife and a mother for his child because he wanted her, but it seemed they were only sharing their stories, not their hearts.

She cursed herself for letting herself fall in love with this man so quickly, for imagining a life with him and their children after only a couple of days. After one afternoon of conversation. A conversation she had completely misunderstood.

She stood there, so quiet and still, fearing that if she spoke or moved she might break into little pieces and crumble before him. Surely her heart was breaking, but she wondered if it showed on her face.

"Do you truly understand, Lady Tremaine? Because I do so want my intentions to be clear."

"Oh your intentions are perfectly clear, Sir Richard," she said, wanting nothing more than to be out of his company. She couldn't believe she had let her heart become entangled with this man's. She wanted to scream, "But I'm in love with you! I thought you were going to ask me to marry you!" But that sort of thing just wasn't done, especially not in Lady Hackle's garden right outside of a sitting room filled with lords and ladies. She would be a laughingstock. And now she found herself having to go into the dinner party on the arm of a man who had just broken her heart.

She hated the idea of having to explain all this to Lady Hackle. And she was angry with her friend for encouraging her to fall for this man so quickly. In that moment all she wanted to do was run away, but instead she stood there, passive as ever, just waiting to see what he would say.

"Very well, I think we should go in to dinner then. I am so relieved we are of the same mind," he said.

She decided then and there she needed to protect her heart, and she was happy she was wearing the brooch her husband had given her, because if she hadn't been, the blow from Sir Richard would have shattered her.

As they walked back into the drawing room and took their places among the assembled guests still waiting to go into dinner, she felt a cold, steely shiver move through her as she touched her brooch. The feeling stayed with her as they sat down at the dining room table, and she imagined it helped her not to cry and make a fool of herself in front of Sir Richard and the other guests.

She could see that Lady Hackle was concerned for her, but of course they wouldn't be able to talk until after dinner, and even then it would be hard for the two of them to find some time to chat among themselves.

And then the strangest thing happened. Lady Hackle and Sir Richard seemed to exchange knowing looks, which made Lady Hackle smile, and she stood up, asking for the party's attention.

"It is with great pleasure that I announce the engagement of my closest friend Lady Tremaine and Sir Richard of the Many Kingdoms! May they both be truly happy as they join their families—Lady Tremaine's daughters, Anastasia and Drizella, with Sir Richard's daughter, Cinderella. Everyone, raise your glasses to Lady Tremaine and Sir Richard!"

Lady Tremaine sat there in shock as everyone

raised their glasses to celebrate their engagement. And she realized her heart didn't need protecting after all. She and her daughters were going to live happily ever after, just as her friend Lady Hackle had wished.

Chapter VII

Mrs. Bramble's Warning

Lady Tremaine's head was spinning after the dinner party. The evening already swirled in her memory like a dream. She tried to hold on to every moment, to form a clear memory she should cherish forever, but it slipped through her fingers, leaving her with fragments. She could hardly believe it was all happening, and so quickly. One moment she thought it was all a misunderstanding, and the next they were engaged.

After dinner Lady Hackle arranged for champagne, chocolates, and fruit in the library so Lady Tremaine and Sir Richard could have a few moments alone before he sailed to the Many Kingdoms.

"I'm sorry to dash off like this, when we have so much left to discuss, but I have been summoned by my king, and it's my duty to attend to him the moment I'm called to his side. It is my express wish, however, that you and your daughters join me as soon as you are able," he said, kissing her hand. "I hope you understand."

She wanted to say she did, but she didn't.

"Won't you come back with me to the Many Kingdoms now? I hate the idea of delaying your journey any longer than necessary." He kissed her hand again, then squeezed it in his own.

"And what of my girls, Richard? I can't go ahead without them." Lady Tremaine shook her head. "Of course I'll leave Lady Hackle's immediately so I can join you as soon as possible, but this is all happening so quickly. There are things that must be considered, plans to be made. My household needs to be packed and shipped, and there is the matter of my servants. I will have to arrange passage for them, as well as for myself and my girls.

My goodness, I have to tell the girls! They're going to be blindsided," she said as Sir Richard took her other hand in his.

"There is no need to bring anything other than your personal belongings, Lady Tremaine. My château is beautifully furnished and fully staffed. Bring your lady's maid and governess for company for you and your girls during the journey, if you wish, but we won't be in need of them once you are settled into your new home. But come quickly and with haste. I need you by my side," he said, looking deeply into her eyes.

Just then there was a knock at the door, and Sir Richard's valet entered. "Excuse me, but we must be going. Sir Richard's carriage must depart now if he's to make the ship to the Many Kingdoms."

"Very well, I'll be there in a moment," Sir Richard said.

"I'd better be off. My king needs me," he said, squeezing her hands a little tighter. Lady Tremaine thought in that moment he would kiss her. They were engaged, after all. It could hardly be inappropriate, they had both married before, and she was no maiden. She closed her eyes waiting for it, and then she felt his lips chastely brush her forehead.

"Goodbye, my dear. Come to me quickly. I can't wait for you to be my wife," he said.

She stood there looking into his eyes, and wondered still if he loved her. Perhaps he was uncomfortable kissing her in front of the valet. She wanted to ask, but couldn't bring herself to.

⚜ ⚜ ⚜ ⚜

Lady Tremaine went up to her room and collapsed onto the bed with a deep sigh. She lay there in the dark trying to catch her breath but was startled by a familiar gravelly voice coming from the corner of the room.

"I see you are already besotted by your prince, and you have forgotten all about your poor Mrs. Bramble."

Lady Tremaine shot up out of bed. She didn't know how she had missed her before, but now she could make out Mrs. Bramble's silhouette, in a velvet chair by the window. The moonlight shone on her wild silver hair and cast shadows on her face, making her look like an old crone from a fairy tale.

"He's not a prince," said Lady Tremaine, standing up and straightening her dress. "He's a knight. And of course I have not forgotten about you, Mrs. Bramble. How are you feeling?" She made her way over to the poor woman.

"I'm in a sorry state. Alone in the world without a friend," Mrs. Bramble said, her eyes watery and yellow from age.

"You are not alone, Mrs. Bramble. You have me," said Lady Tremaine.

"You don't need me anymore. You're sending me away, don't you deny it. The witches' girl told me so. It's clear she and your fairy tale prince have you in their clutches."

Lady Tremaine kneeled down so she could look her in the eye. "Stop this now. What's this talk of witches? I am in no one's clutches," she said. She was sorry to see Mrs. Bramble in such a state.

"Rebecca said you're sending me to live with my

sister," said Mrs. Bramble. "And that you're moving to the Many Kingdoms."

Lady Tremaine shook her head. "Well, I can hardly say how she would know I was going to the Many Kingdoms when I have just decided to go myself."

Mrs. Bramble cackled. It was an ugly, raspy laugh that made Lady Tremaine's teeth itch. "Oh, you knew you were going off with him the moment you laid eyes on him! You're already under their spell. You were always a fool for a handsome face and a fat purse," she said, laughing again.

"Now that is enough!" Lady Tremaine got up and walked to the center of the room. "I don't know what's come over you, Mrs. Bramble, but you must pull yourself together. I won't have you speaking to me like this," she said, pulling the cord to call Rebecca.

"Mark my words, dearie, you will regret it if you go to the Many Kingdoms. Please just read the book of fairy tales I gave you, it's all in there. Then you will see why I am so worried about you," said Mrs. Bramble with imploring eyes.

"I wish there was something I could say to ease your mind, Mrs. Bramble." Lady Tremaine eyed the door, waiting for Rebecca to knock and put an end to this conversation. "I assure you I will be very happy with Sir Richard." She was worried for the woman's state of mind.

"There is a special bond between a nanny and her charge, as you will learn in the pages of that book. I've always seen you very clearly, and I know beyond a doubt that something horrible will happen if you leave."

Lady Tremaine took her hand. She wondered if the poor dear wasn't suffering from some sort of dementia from old age.

"Why are you so convinced something terrible will happen to me?" she asked. "Why do you think someone will hurt me?" She searched the old woman's face, wondering what made her look so heart-stricken.

"I'm not worried you will be hurt, my little one. You're a strong woman, and you can handle anything those witches try to cast your way," said Mrs. Bramble.

"Then what has you so worried? What are you so afraid of?" asked Lady Tremaine, and the strangest look came over Mrs. Bramble's face.

"Oh, my dear, don't you see, I'm worried about those *you* may hurt, those you will destroy with your hate and cruelty."

Rebecca walked into the room just then and heard what Mrs. Bramble said. "That's utter nonsense. My lady doesn't have a cruel bone in her body," Rebecca said.

"Oh, your lady will after you and your witches are done with her!" Mrs. Bramble croaked. "It happens to all of them! Something is terribly wrong with the Many Kingdoms. It turns stepmothers into horrible monsters. It destroys everything good within them." Mrs. Bramble grabbed the book of fairy tales from the table beside her. "Just read this, my lady. Read it before you make the biggest mistake of your life."

Lady Tremaine took the book and smiled at the old woman. "I will read it. I promise," she said, trying to make the woman happy and opening the book.

"What's this, an inscription from Lord Tremaine?" she said, taking a closer look. "You got this book from Lord Tremaine's library? Why didn't you say so from the start?" Lady Tremaine asked.

"I thought you knew, my lady. He mentioned he bought it at the same shop as your brooch. Lord Tremaine always let the staff borrow his books, my lady, as long as we logged it in his ledger," said Mrs. Bramble.

Lady Tremaine knew this was true, of course. This conversation, combined with the events from the last few days, had her head spinning in circles. "Well, then I am even happier to have it in my possession, Mrs. Bramble. I will take extra care to read it. Thank you so much for giving it back."

Lady Tremaine motioned to Rebecca to take the old woman out of the room. "Now, you go back downstairs with Rebecca and stay there and rest until I send for you. Everything will be well, I promise you," she said, kissing Mrs. Bramble on the cheek.

She took a deep breath once both ladies were out of the room. "Good grief," she said, looking at the book. Seeing Lord Tremaine's handwriting sent a wave of love and sadness through her. She never knew he had gone back to that strange little shop for the book. She remembered the proprietor mentioning it, and she thought it sounded just like something her husband would do, going back to the shop to get it. But she hated the ideas and notions this book had put in Mrs. Bramble's mind. The old woman had clearly convinced herself that the stories were true. And then she remembered her conversation with Sir Richard about whether the book of fairy tales could be a history. Could the stories be true after all?

Rebecca came back into the room, interrupting

her thoughts. "Sit down, my lady, you look pale," she said, holding out a chair for Lady Tremaine.

"Thank you, Rebecca dear. Do you know much about the Many Kingdoms? I swear I remember Sir Richard saying something about a book of fairy tales." She put her hand to her head, and Rebecca took the book from her.

"Don't worry about that now. I'm sure they are different books. Why don't you lie down? It's been a long day, and tomorrow will be another one. You need your rest."

⚜ ⚜ ⚜ ⚜

The next morning was spent in a flurry of excitement. As soon as she finished her coffee and was dressed, Lady Tremaine found herself surrounded by a legion of maids, all assisting Rebecca in packing her things so she could make her way back to London to tell her girls the news. She had written ahead to let her butler, Avery, know she was on her way. He was to instruct the servants to pack up the household and to tell Nanny Pinch to ready the girls for a long journey.

Lady Tremaine's head was whirling with everything she had to do, and with everything she and Sir Richard had discussed the night before. He was right to suggest she only bring her personal belongings. It was an extraordinarily long journey to the Many Kingdoms, after all, and it wasn't sensible to bring everything with her, including her servants.

Thank goodness for Rebecca, who was fussing around the room, directing Lady Hackle's staff in the packing of Lady Tremaine's trunks so she could make her way home on the next train. Lady Tremaine was eager to be reunited with Anastasia and Drizella as soon as possible so she could share the good news.

"Rebecca, once we're back in London I want you to supervise the packing of my personal belongings. Dresses, hats, gloves, jewelry, purses, some of my favorite books, and of course the contents of my vanity. Everything else will have to be put into crates and auctioned off. I'll need you to oversee all of that as well. I will have my hands full breaking the news to the girls and meeting with my solicitor so we can arrange the sale of the town house," said Lady Tremaine.

"Of course, my lady. And what of Miss Anastasia and Miss Drizella's things? Shall I pack for them as well?" she asked.

"No, Nanny Pinch will see to that. I've written ahead. And, Rebecca, I need you to work closely with my butler, Avery, to make sure everything is done to my specifications."

Rebecca stopped what she was doing. "How will Avery and the other servants feel about me swooping in and taking charge like that, my lady? Will they be upset about Mrs. Bramble?"

Lady Tremaine hadn't even thought of that. "Well, Avery is a good sort, but if he does get his nose out of joint, there is nothing we can do." She continued, "Oh, Rebecca, there is so much to do. And I have to break it to the staff that I won't be needing them." She was starting to feel faint.

"My lady, please sit down," Rebecca said. "I think you might swoon from all the excitement. I wouldn't worry about your staff. I can't imagine they'd want to travel so far anyway." She had stopped directing the maids in order to give Lady Tremaine her full attention.

"Yes, I think you're right. Though I do hope Nanny Pinch comes along, even if just for the first few months." She sat down in a pink velvet chair situated near a window with a little round table beside it.

"Shall I send down for some tea?" Rebecca asked.

"I know you mean well, always suggesting tea, but if you're going to be my lady's maid, remember, never tea, Rebecca, always coffee. I know that's not very English of me, but I've always preferred it."

Rebecca nodded. "Yes, my lady. I should have remembered." She motioned to one of the maids to fetch her lady some coffee.

There was a knock at the door. "Ah, I suppose that couldn't be my coffee already?" said Lady Tremaine, laughing.

"No, my lady. We're still in England, where things don't magically appear as they do in the Many Kingdoms." Rebecca smiled as she opened the door to Lady Hackle. Lady Tremaine's friend stood there with a look of grave concern on her face.

"My friend, this letter came for you just now. It's from Sir Richard. He must have sent it right before his ship disembarked."

Lady Tremaine took the letter from her friend and read it.

My dearest Lady Tremaine,

I can't wait another moment for us to be husband and wife. Please come to me as quickly as you can, for I am desperate for you to take your place at my side, and in my home. If you love me as much as I hope you do, you will bring Anastasia and Drizella on the next evening voyage. Cinderella and I need you.

Sir Richard

Lady Tremaine handed the letter back to her friend so she could read it.

"Oh, you have to go to him at once," Lady Hackle said.

"But I'm already leaving as quickly as I can.

What of the house in London?" Lady Tremaine was distraught. "What about the girls? I haven't even told them we are moving, and I must book us all on the next evening voyage?"

Lady Hackle looked off for a moment as if she was formulating a plan. "Nanny Pinch will just have to bring them to the dock. Hopefully she will agree to come along with you to the Many Kingdoms, but if she doesn't, the least she can do is bring your girls to meet you at the boat. Your new family needs you. If you had any doubt of his feelings of love toward you, this surely squelches that," she said.

"I think you're right, but what of the house and the servants? There is so much to do." She took a cup of coffee from a tray that had been brought in by one of the maids.

"The ship isn't leaving the dock until this evening. That should give Nanny Pinch enough time to get some things together for you and the girls. Piggy and I will go to your place in London tomorrow and supervise everything else and arrange to have the rest of your things shipped to the Many Kingdoms," said Lady Hackle.

Lady Tremaine took her friend's hand. "You're such a good friend, Prudence. Thank you." She laughed.

"It's nothing, dear friend; it's just a matter of directing your servants. Will you pay them a severance? Should we double the usual under the circumstances?" She continued, "And what about the house and the things to be auctioned? Is your solicitor handling that? Should Piggy and I stop by his office when I'm in London to make the arrangements for you?"

Lady Tremaine started to panic. There was so much to be done, and here she was dashing off before she could sort any of it out. "Oh, Prudence, would you handle all that, really? I'm afraid I am asking too much of you, my sweet friend, but I have no choice."

Lady Hackle laughed. "It's for the best possible reason. You're sailing off to be with your love!" she said, smiling.

"This is all happening so quickly. I wanted time to talk with the girls before rushing off to lands unknown," said Lady Tremaine, motioning to one of the servants for another cup of coffee.

Lady Hackle put her hands on her friend's shoulders tenderly. "You can talk to the girls on the ship. Listen to me, my friend, you are the strongest woman I know. You can do this. You're finally going to have your happily ever after, in the land of fairy tales. This is a dream come true."

Chapter VIII

The Marvelous Adventure

Lady Tremaine stood nervously on the dock, waiting for Nanny Pinch, Anastasia, and Drizella to arrive. She kept looking at her watch pendent, worried they wouldn't make it to the dock in time.

It was a grand and beautiful ship, all white and gold, reminding her of a many-tiered wedding cake. Every time the ship's horn blasted she jumped, thinking it meant they were about to ring out the last call for passengers to board, but logically she knew they had plenty of time. Her nerves were such a jumble.

She had at least managed to arrange two very

fine staterooms, one for herself, and some rather large quarters for Nanny Pinch, Rebecca, and the girls—all adjoining, of course.

As she stood there, she felt like she was in a dream. It didn't seem real, the thought of leaving her entire household without seeing it again, or without saying goodbye to those who had cared for her for so many years. She had gone straight from the train to the dock. She would have been more upset, but it was all terribly romantic, the idea of her dearest love, so desperate to have her at his side that he asked her to dash it all and come to him as quickly as she could.

Just then she saw her precious girls and Nanny Pinch approaching in the carriage. Her girls were waving frantically, smiling, and eager to bolt out of the carriage. The moment it pulled to a stop, they climbed over Nanny Pinch and bolted from the carriage, running straight into Lady Tremaine's arms.

"Oh, Mama, we missed you so much!" cried Anastasia.

"We promise to be good from now on!" said Drizella, squeezing her mother tightly.

Lady Tremaine was so happy to see her daughters. Seeing them made everything seem more real to her. They were the center of her universe, and she felt untethered without them.

"Hello, my darlings! I am so happy to see you," she said, giving them both kisses. "And thank you, Nanny Pinch. You have no idea how much I appreciate you agreeing to come along with us to the Many Kingdoms."

"I'm sorry I won't be able to stay with you longer than the first fortnight to see the girls settled," Nanny Pinch said, "but Lady Hackle explained everything, and I couldn't let you and the girls travel alone all the way to the Many Kingdoms."

Lady Tremaine gave the young woman a smile. "Oh, but we won't be entirely alone. Rebecca will also be traveling with us. She is my new lady's maid. You will meet her on the ship. She is in our rooms making sure everything is satisfactory."

Lady Tremaine reached for her daughters. "Come, Anastasia and Drizella," she said. "Take my hands. We are about to embark on a marvelous adventure."

⚜ ⚜ ⚜ ⚜

Lady Tremaine and her daughters sat together in a little sitting area in her stateroom, while Rebecca and Nanny Pinch unpacked their things in the adjoining room they would share with Drizella and Anastasia. The girls were on either side of her, as close as they could manage. She could tell they had missed her, and she, too, had missed them terribly.

"My angels, what did Nanny Pinch tell you about our journey?"

Anastasia spoke first. "She said we were going to a magical land with princes and princesses."

Drizella scoffed. "We have princesses in England; I don't see how that's magical," she said.

Lady Tremaine laughed. "That's true, my dear, but it seems the Many Kingdoms has far more royalty than London. I am told we are moving to a kingdom with a very jolly king and his son, the young prince who is about your age. Who knows, maybe one day one of you will marry him," she teased.

"But what of Shrimpy and Dicky? I thought we were to marry them!" said Anastasia.

Lady Tremaine grabbed their hands and kissed them. "Well, of course you will, darlings. I'm just teasing. We will arrange for you to visit Shrimpy and Dicky as soon as we are settled in our new home. You were very missed at the house party, and I bet the boys are eager to see you," she said. But she wondered how she felt about her girls being so very far away from her, all the way back in London, once they were married.

She and Lady Hackle had had it all worked out, their future set. Their children would marry and they would be grandmothers together. Perhaps they would still have their dream, though she could no longer see it as clearly as before.

"Maybe we can talk Lady Prudence into spending the season in the Many Kingdoms with the boys. I'm sure they have coming-out balls there just as they do in England," said Lady Tremaine.

Drizella's eyes grew wide. "Oh! Imagine! There must be so many more courts in which to be presented. Oh, yes, Mama, I think this is an excellent plan!" she said.

"Now," said Lady Tremaine, "what did Nanny Pinch tell you about our marvelous adventure? Did she tell you that I am to be married to a lovely man named Sir Richard and that he has a daughter around your age, with whom I am sure you will become great friends? Did she tell you we are to live with them in their beautiful château?" Lady Tremaine held her breath, wondering how her girls would react to the news.

"Yes, Mama," said Anastasia. "Which part of the Many Kingdoms is this? If it is to be our new home, shouldn't we know what to call it?"

Lady Tremaine realized with a start that she didn't know.

Just then Rebecca and Nanny Pinch came into the room.

"Hello, dears. Anastasia has made me realize that, in all this rush, I have no idea in what realm in the Many Kingdoms we will be living. Isn't that ridiculous?" she said, slightly embarrassed.

Rebecca and Nanny Pinch sat down across from the trio.

"You will be living in King Hubert's lands, not far from where the Beast King and Queen Belle reside," Rebecca said.

Lady Tremaine raised her eyebrow. "You seem to know a lot about the Many Kingdoms, Rebecca," she said.

"Yes, my lady. I assumed Lady Prudence told you that is where I am from."

Lady Tremaine started. She couldn't help flashing back to her last conversation with Mrs. Bramble and the old woman's warning. But before she could ask anything further, she realized Anastasia and Drizella looked frightened.

"What's the matter, girls? Why are you upset?" asked Lady Tremaine.

"Beast King?" asked Drizella. "What is a Beast

King? I don't want to live in a kingdom ruled by an ugly old beast!"

Nanny Pinch raised her hand for silence. "Now, Drizella. Remember what we talked about. Think about how you'd like to rephrase that."

Rebecca laughed. "Oh, that's not necessary. He was an ugly old beast, or at least some thought so, but now he's a beautiful king living his happily ever after with his true love, Queen Belle. And you won't be living in their kingdom anyway. Theirs is the next kingdom over from ours. Kingdoms don't usually intermingle so your paths will never cross. Don't worry."

Anastasia was confused. "What do you mean the king was living his happily ever after? Isn't that what fairy tale authors usually say about the princess once she is saved by her prince?"

Rebecca laughed again. "Well, in this story it was the princess who saved the prince. Belle is the hero of that story." Drizella and Anastasia clapped their hands.

"Oh, I like that! I would like to meet Queen Belle!" said Drizella. "Oh, Mama, you're taking us to the most magnificent place. Thank you." She kissed her mother on the cheek.

Lady Tremaine smiled and yawned.

"Come now, girls," Nanny Pinch said, standing up. "Your mama is tired, and I think it's time to let her rest." She took each girl by the hand and led them into the adjoining room.

"I love you, my darlings," said Lady Tremaine, blowing them a kiss. "I will see you later at dinner." She was so happy her daughters were excited about this journey. "Rebecca, you stay with me for a while," she said when they were alone. "What did you do with that book of fairy tales? I would like to read it on our journey to the Many Kingdoms."

Rebecca cast her eyes downward. "I'm sorry, my lady. It's in the crates down in cargo. I can find it for you the moment we get to the Many Kingdoms, as soon as I am able to unpack."

Lady Tremaine signed. "Very well, then I am afraid you will have to answer all of my daughters' and my questions about the Many Kingdoms for as long as this voyage takes."

Rebecca laughed. "It would be my pleasure, my lady."

CHAPTER IX

THE MANY KINGDOMS

When the ladies disembarked from their ship after their unbearably long journey, it felt to Lady Tremaine as if they had indeed stepped into another world. She was so relieved to be on land again and hoped her life in the Many Kingdoms was worth the voyage. She decided almost at once it might be. She marveled at her surroundings, dazzled by the magnificent lighthouse, its Fresnel lens glistening in the sunlight.

"What kingdom is this, Rebecca?" she asked, looking up at the grandest lighthouse she had ever seen. "This place is remarkable." She took her girls by the hands, leaving Nanny Pinch to find a porter to take their luggage to the carriage Sir Richard had arranged to be waiting for them.

"This is Morningstar Kingdom, my lady," said Rebecca. "It is one of the major port kingdoms. And that, my lady, is the Lighthouse of the Gods," said Rebecca, motioning to the Cyclopean tower, which looked as if it indeed had been built by gods and not humans.

Lady Tremaine and her daughters were awe-struck by its beauty. They stood there speechless, almost bewitched by the diamond-like lens in the tower. "Who could have built such a lighthouse?" she asked, her eyes wide.

"It was built by the Cyclopean Giants that used to rule this part of the land before the Morningstars, who built their castle to complement the lighthouse's design," Rebecca said. "The Lighthouse of the Gods has cast its protective eye over countless ships for more years than almost anyone can recollect." Rebecca was clearly happy to see her lady so pleased with her new surroundings.

Lady Tremaine felt a thrill to be in such a

beautiful land, and one even older than England. Morningstar Castle was exquisitely perched on the highest rocky cliffs overlooking the ocean. She wondered if her new home would have such a breathtaking view.

"I'm sorry, my lady." Rebecca interrupted her reverie. "We must be going. It looks like Nanny Pinch found us a porter. Shall we all head to the carriage? It's a long journey still to King Hubert's lands." Rebecca led Lady Tremaine and her daughters to the carriage. It was a lovely white carriage trimmed in gold, pulled by two massive white stallions with yellow plumes on their heads. Lady Tremaine was impressed that her betrothed had arranged such a stately ride for her and her daughters. After seeing Morningstar Castle and now riding in such a fine carriage, she had high hopes for what she might find once she finally reached her new home.

Lady Tremaine and her daughters snuggled into one side of the carriage, and Rebecca and Nanny Pinch sat on the other. Their personal luggage was piled on the back, and their crated items were put into a wagon that followed them at its own leisurely pace.

All the ladies chatted happily as they passed through the majestic yet terrifying Cyclopean Mountains. They had never seen mountains so tall and craggy, and imagined the legendary giants traversing them with ease as Sir Richard's horse-drawn carriage slowly made its way down the winding path. They passed through several kingdoms on their way to their new home, including one with a tall stone tower where a young girl with long golden magical hair was rumored to be held captive. And as if that wasn't frightening enough, they passed the largest cemetery they had ever seen surrounded by a thicket of dead rosebushes. It gave Lady Tremaine and her daughters chills as they passed it. Even though it was an eerie place, Lady Tremaine saw the beauty in it, with its tall stone mansion, glistening solariums, weeping angels, and wild beasts carved of stone.

"That is the Dead Woods," said Rebecca. "That is where the queen of the dead has ruled for longer than anyone recalls." Her words made Lady

Tremaine, her daughters, and Nanny Pinch shudder. Lady Tremaine was wondering what kind of place she had brought her daughters to. A place where witches hid young girls in towers, and there were queens who ruled over the dead. But they found themselves in their own corner of the Many Kingdoms at last.

"Look, girls," Rebecca said, pointing as they passed Queen Belle's castle. "That's where the Beast King lives. That means we are almost home."

"I wonder if we will see him," said Anastasia with breathless excitement. But the moment they crested the mountain that separated Queen Belle's kingdom from theirs, all thoughts of Belle were forgotten. They were home at last.

"Oh, Mama! Look at that castle! Is that where we are going to live?" asked Drizella, leaning out the carriage window to get a better look at King Hubert's castle.

"No, my darling, that is where the royal family lives," Lady Tremaine said, thinking it was the most beautiful castle she had ever seen. It looked as if it were straight out of a fairy tale, with its tall turrets and golden spires, all pastel blue with gilded trim. She had never seen so many towers. It didn't look or feel as ancient as Morningstar Castle; it wasn't awe-inspiring in that way, but it was, in Lady Tremaine's opinion, much more elegant.

"Mama! The tops of those towers look like blue witch's caps!" squealed Anastasia, pointing at one of the towers and leaning so far out the carriage window that Nanny Pinch had to yank her back inside.

"I suppose they do," said Lady Tremaine, hardly noticing the minor commotion. She was remembering Mrs. Bramble's ominous warnings about witches. She still wondered if she had made the right choice in asking Lady Hackle to arrange to have Mrs. Bramble live with her sister, and decided she would ask Nanny Pinch to look in on her when she got back to England.

Just then the carriage stopped. "My ladies, look, it's your new home," said Rebecca.

Lady Tremaine wasn't sure what she was expecting, but her new home seemed to pale in comparison to what she had imagined. It was a lovely enough stone château, with a single tower and tall windows. She supposed it was a grand house in its own way, though not quite as lovely as her home in London. She let out a deep sigh and decided there was nothing to be done about it. This was her new home, and she'd better decide to find things about it she loved. She stood there looking at it, deciding she must be happy here. She needed to make it her home, a place to live and love, and have her happily ever after.

"Look, Mama, our house has a witch's cap tower, too!" said Drizella.

Lady Tremaine had expected to see Sir Richard and Cinderella standing on the porch waiting for them, but they were nowhere in sight. In fact, no one was there to greet them at all.

"Has no one come to meet us, then?" said Lady Tremaine, worrying that perhaps they had arrived at the wrong estate.

"Not to worry, my lady. I will alert the staff that we are here. I am sure Sir Richard and Cinderella will come right out once they know we have arrived.

Please wait here, I won't be more than a moment," Rebecca said, and dashed off to the front door to ring the bell.

An older, round-faced woman with white hair answered the door and let Rebecca in. It seemed like Rebecca was in the house for an eternity, and Lady Tremaine hardly knew what to do. It was unheard of not to greet your guests when they arrived, let alone your new family. She rapped her fingers on the side of the carriage nervously, waiting until she finally saw Sir Richard emerge from within.

"Lady Tremaine! You are finally here! Thank goodness," he said, running to the carriage and opening the door for her. "Come! Come inside, all of you. We have been waiting for you." He held the carriage door for them. "And you must be Anastasia and Drizella," he said, looking at them both intensely, almost appraisingly. "You have a beauty unlike any other in the Many Kingdoms." Anastasia and Drizella giggled as they stepped from the carriage. "Ah, and here is the lady of the house.

Welcome, my dear lady." He kissed her hand like the gallant knight he was. Lady Tremaine's spirits rose at this chivalrous display.

"You know my lady's maid, Rebecca," she said. "And this is Nanny Pinch. She is here to see the girls settled before she goes back to England."

"Welcome, all of you. Now come, Cinderella is waiting to meet you, but we don't have much time before we are due at the chapel. I told the vicar we would be there well before now, but I suppose your journey was delayed," he said, ushering the ladies to the front door.

Lady Tremaine's head spun. "I hadn't realized we were late," she said, her heart sinking. "Are we to be wed today? The dress I had planned to wear—the rest of our belongings—everything is still in the second carriage, which hasn't arrived yet." She looked down the path as if hoping to see it coming over the crest at that moment.

"Well, my darling, I can't install an unmarried woman who isn't a servant into my house," he said.

"We must be married today, there is no way around it. Ah, look! There is Cinderella now."

Lady Tremaine followed his gaze to the girl who emerged through the front doors. She thought she was the prettiest little thing she had ever seen. She could see Sir Richard hadn't exaggerated about his daughter's beauty. What was it about the Many Kingdoms that produced such fine-looking people? First Sir Richard and now his daughter. Even Rebecca was remarkably beautiful with her chestnut hair and large hazel eyes, and Lady Tremaine wondered if everyone in the Many Kingdoms was as striking as the present company.

She gave her own daughters a sideways glance, recognizing the envy mounting within them as soon as they saw Cinderella. She decided to cut the tension by introducing herself to the angelic girl.

"Cinderella, I am your new mama, and these are your sisters, Anastasia and Drizella. I hope we will all be happy here together," said Lady Tremaine, smiling at the glowing young lady.

Cinderella took a step forward, beaming.

"Welcome to my mother's home, Lady Tremaine," she said, smiling at her new stepmother.

Cinderella's words stung Lady Tremaine's heart and took her by surprise. "It would please me if you could find it in your heart to call me Mama," she said. "Because I so want to be a good mama to you." Lady Tremaine tried to keep her face calm, so as not to let the young girl know she had crushed her heart.

"I can call you Stepmother if you'd like," the girl replied. "Papa said I may call you Lady Tremaine or Stepmother, but never Mama."

Lady Tremaine's heart fell, but she didn't let Cinderella or her father know it. This girl simply didn't understand that what she was saying was hurtful. Lady Tremaine had to wonder if Cinderella had been so sheltered, so kept from society that she didn't know how to conduct herself in polite company? Well, it seemed Lady Tremaine had her work cut out for her.

"Very well, Cinderella. You may call me Stepmother if that is what pleases you and your papa," she said, though she intended to speak with Sir Richard about this later. She realized they hadn't spoken of these things while they were at Lady Hackle's, but she assumed they would be a true family. Perhaps Cinderella and her father just needed a bit of time?

Lady Tremaine could see her girls getting twitchy at Cinderella's treatment of her and thought it was best to usher them to their rooms before they pounced on their fair-haired beauty of a stepsister, but just as she was about to say it was time they all go refresh themselves, Anastasia spoke.

"My mama is trying to be your friend, Cinderella. Why are you being so rude?" she said.

Then Drizella chimed in. "Oh, Stasia, we can hardly blame Cinderella, considering she has such a rude father. We came all this way and he didn't even greet us—ow!"

Nanny Pinch had grabbed Drizella by the arm and was pulling her toward her. "Drizella, how dare you speak about your new papa like that?" she said, tightening her grip on Drizella's arm.

"Now that's enough, the both of you!" said Lady Tremaine, her face undoubtedly red. "Please excuse us, Sir Richard. We have had a very long journey, and the girls are exhausted. If someone could please show us to our rooms, I will help the girls get ready for the ceremony." She looked around in vain for the servants.

"Nanny Pinch, you will find the girls' rooms on the third landing," Sir Richard said. "They will take the first and second from the stairway. Lady Tremaine's room is the third."

Lady Tremaine thought this was all highly unusual. She wondered where the servants could be. Would they be expected to simply wander the third landing until they found their rooms themselves?

"Rebecca," Sir Richard continued. "You can take Lady Tremaine's things up to her room, while Nanny Pinch sees the girls settled into theirs. Lady Tremaine and I have to go directly to the chapel."

Lady Tremaine flinched. "Right now, this moment? But I've not even changed. And what about the girls? Won't they be joining us?"

Sir Richard took her hand. "I'm sure you would agree the girls are in no disposition for an excursion, my dear. Besides, this will be my last chance to have you to myself for a while. Would you deny me that?" He kissed her hand again.

This all seemed so strange to her. She couldn't put her finger on it, but it just didn't feel right, and in that moment, when his lips brushed her hand, something within her told her to flee.

She hardly knew what to say. The last thing she wanted to do was get married right after such a long journey. But she supposed it couldn't be helped. Sir Richard must have worried it would be a scandal if she moved in before they were married.

She wished she had known this on the journey over. She would have worn something more appropriate for a wedding. As it was, she had chosen one of her more austere dark purple dresses over a high-collared lilac blouse that she accented with her favorite jade brooch. A very respectable outfit but not one befitting a festive occasion, especially not her own wedding.

"Very well, Sir Richard," she said. "But you will have to excuse me for just a moment while I quickly refresh myself. Come along, ladies," she said as she headed up the stairs, followed by Nanny Pinch, Rebecca, and her daughters. The minute they reached the third landing her girls started protesting.

"Mama, I don't like it here," Anastasia whined. "This is a sad, gloomy house, and that Cinderella is a beast!"

Lady Tremaine agreed, but she held her tongue. The house was rather dark and a bit dingy, and the furniture, though likely very beautiful in its day, had become threadbare and lackluster. She felt she really should have brought her own things rather than selling them off; now she was going to have to buy all new furniture for this house. And where were the servants? It didn't make sense. None of it did really, but she reasoned she was exhausted and probably making more of everything because she had gotten such little sleep on their long journey.

"Yes, Mama! And why won't Sir Richard let us come to the wedding?" Drizella complained.

Lady Tremaine couldn't help agreeing with her daughters, but she felt tiredness was clouding all of their judgment. "My dears, we are all of us so tired from our long carriage ride here, not to mention the journey by sea. Perhaps Sir Richard is right, and you three girls can stay here and get to know one another while we go to the chapel. I bet he has a grand party planned for afterward and that is why we have not seen any of the servants. I bet they are all working on it and planning a splendid surprise for us. We will all get to celebrate together then. Perhaps after you've changed you can sneak down to the kitchens and spy on what they may be up to? I bet you'll see a large wedding cake and all sorts of delicious things to eat." It all sounded so lovely that Lady Tremaine almost believed it herself. "Don't fret, my girls. I know Cinderella and her papa didn't make the best first impression, but I imagine they are both just as nervous as we are. I am sure that in no time we will all be great friends," she said cheerfully.

The girls looked hopeful, but unconvinced.

"Well put, my lady," said Rebecca. "Now let's get you ready for your big day." With that, she led Lady Tremaine off to her room, leaving the girls feeling bewildered and alone.

Chapter X

Lady of the House

The wedding was a whirlwind. The vicar had been waiting for them in his tiny white chapel, and rather impatiently at that. He hurried the ceremony, had them sign the papers with his wife as witness, and it was done. Just like that. There were no rose petals, no kisses, no cake. No one had thought to decorate the chapel or arrange for a bundle of flowers for her to hold. No friends or family cheering for them as they walked back down the aisle as husband and wife. She felt like an afterthought, and remarkably alone.

It all seemed like a formality, not at all what she had expected.

Once they were outside the chapel, a royal carriage was waiting alongside their own, and Lady Tremaine wondered, her heart full of hope, if perhaps Sir Richard didn't have something grand planned for them after all.

"Ah, it's the Grand Duke," he said. "Come, my lady, let me introduce you." Sir Richard rushed them over to the carriage, where a lanky man stood, sporting a formal gray livery and an elaborate mustache that reminded Lady Tremaine of a writhing serpent.

"Grand Duke, this is Lady Tremaine, my new wife."

The duke wrinkled his nose, which made his mustache quiver. "So you've finally done the deed. Very good, man. The king expects you immediately. I assume you have all the paperwork, signed and ready?" he asked.

"I do, Grand Duke," said Sir Richard.

"Very well, then you may ride with me to the castle. It was lovely meeting you, Lady Tremaine. I will send your regards to the king," he said snottily, which made Lady Tremaine flinch. She had hardly had a moment to say a word, let alone send her regards to the king. Here she was already making the worst of impressions.

"Things are done so strangely here, my love. Must you rush off to register our wedding papers now? I wish you could come back home with me to celebrate rather than go straight to the castle." She gathered from the look on his face that this was not to be the case, so she added, "But if you must go, then please let us depart with a kiss." She moved toward him, but he flinched and backed away from her.

"Lady, please!" he said stiffly. "Not in front of the Grand Duke."

Lady Tremaine flushed, embarrassed. She wondered how many more indignities she would suffer this day. Nothing was at all as she had imagined. As she made her way home in her carriage alone, she wondered how she had gotten herself into this mess. She was exhausted, her wedding had been rushed, and her husband had already started making excuses not to kiss her. She didn't have a good feeling about any of this.

She felt more alone than she had after her first husband had died. At least in England she had had her friends to comfort her. Here she was almost entirely alone.

When she returned to the château, she let herself inside and stood in the vast vestibule. The house was eerily quiet, and she decided she must be right; the servants had to be working on some sort of surprise wedding reception. Still, as she looked around at her new home, Lady Tremaine couldn't help but feel disappointed. The château wasn't as stately as she was expecting. It was a beautiful home, but not quite as grand as her previous home in London, and it was going to take some work to bring it to her usual standards.

Well, she had money enough and planned to do just that the moment she was settled in. If this was going to be her new home, she was going to make it as lovely as possible.

As she stood in the vestibule envisioning all the changes she might make, a squat, round-faced woman, white hair piled into a pristine bun, descended the stairs with a large carpetbag.

"Welcome, Lady Tremaine," she said nervously.

"Thank you, Mrs. . . ." Lady Tremaine paused expectantly.

The old woman turned scarlet. "Yes, I'm so sorry, I'm Mrs. Butterpants, I was head housekeeper, and Cinderella's governess."

Lady Tremaine suppressed a laugh, not missing a beat. "*Was* head housekeeper and governess? Are you leaving, then?" she said, surveying the woman.

"I'm sorry, my lady; I assumed Sir Richard told you. I was informed that my services were no longer needed now that Cinderella has a stepmother."

Lady Tremaine narrowed her eyes, her hand reaching for her brooch for comfort. She thought it was odd, as she was certainly no replacement for a proper governess, but she thought it prudent not to argue, and quite frankly she was much too tired.

"I see, but what will you do, Mrs. Butterpants? Do you have another means of employment lined up?"

The woman smiled. "You're so kind to ask. My brother has a bakery in a neighboring kingdom. I'm sure you passed through it on your way, the one with the very tall tower. I'm going to help him."

Lady Tremaine laughed at the idea of a family of bakers called Butterpants. "Well, good luck then, Mrs. Butterpants. Before you go, may I ask where the other servants are? I was surprised they weren't here to greet me when I arrived."

Mrs. Butterpants turned a deeper shade of scarlet than before. "There are no other servants, Lady Tremaine. I was the last."

Again Lady Tremaine didn't understand, but she chose not to share her displeasure with the old woman.

"I see. Well, Mrs. Butterpants, I'd better not keep you from your journey. I assume Sir Richard has arranged your transportation?"

Mrs. Butterpants scoffed under her breath. "No,

my lady, but not to worry, my brother has sent a horse and cart to collect me. I think it might be waiting for me outside."

Lady Tremaine shook her head. She was not impressed by the way Sir Richard ran his home. She would have her hands full getting this place into order.

"Well, then, Mrs. Butterpants, have a safe journey," she said, feeling completely bewildered.

"Goodbye, Lady Tremaine. Good luck to you," she said as she made her way out the front door. And something about her tone sounded as if she thought Lady Tremaine would need it.

Lady Tremaine just stood there for a moment taking in the size of the place, wondering how it could possibly be managed without a staff. Just then Nanny Pinch came down the stairs looking frantic.

"Lady Tremaine, do you realize there is no staff here whatsoever?"

Lady Tremaine did her best to remain calm,

again reaching for her brooch for comfort. She was happy she had worn it for the journey, because she was feeling she needed an extra layer of protection in this strange new place.

"Yes, Nanny Pinch. I know I only have you for a fortnight before you must go back to London, but could I prevail upon you to stay a bit longer, just while Rebecca and I arrange for a new staff?"

Nanny Pinch looked almost as uncomfortable as Mrs. Butterpants had. "My lady, what am I thinking, speaking with you about servants when you've just returned from your wedding? I'm so sorry. Where is Sir Richard?" she asked, looking around for him.

"He had some business at the castle. Things are done so strangely here, Nanny Pinch. The moment we were married the Grand Duke was there demanding he file our marriage contract with the king," said Lady Tremaine. "But you didn't answer my question. Could you find your way to staying on just a little longer?"

"I'm sorry, my lady. I wish I could stay, but I just can't. I hate the idea of being so far from my mother; it would take ages for me to get home should she need me," said Nanny Pinch, looking sincerely sorry.

Lady Tremaine clenched her fist, wishing she were in London, surrounded by her own servants, in her own home, with beautiful things that she loved, where Nanny Pinch would be happy to stay on.

"I understand, Miss Pinch. I appreciate you agreeing to stay as long as you have already. I know you have to get back to London to your mother. You're a very devoted daughter, and she is lucky to have you. I promise I won't keep you a moment longer than we agreed. Now, I suppose I'd better see how one goes about finding servants in the Many Kingdoms."

Nanny Pinch smiled. "I think Rebecca can help you with that," she said.

"Yes, how clever of you, Nanny Pinch. I knew that girl would be a boon to me. Now I suppose we'd better go upstairs and break it to the girls that there will be no wedding reception this evening."

Not for the first time that day, Lady Tremaine wondered if she had made the right decision, bringing her girls clear across the world where they didn't have a single soul who loved or cared for them.

CHAPTER XI

THE MICE

Lady Tremaine was sitting in her room while Rebecca busily unpacked her things, finding a proper place for everything. The carriage with the rest of their belongings had finally arrived when she and Sir Richard were at the chapel. She sat in a faded green velvet chair near a window that overlooked the courtyard. It was lightly dusted with snow, and Lady Tremaine wondered if her journey to the Many Kingdoms had been longer than she had thought. Surely it hadn't taken more than two months to make their journey. Could it truly be winter already? She found herself musing at how lovely it would be for Anastasia and Drizella to have snow on Christmas, like they might have in London, and with that she felt a little bit more at home. Her things didn't look quite right in her new room. It was cavernous, and rather sparse with furnishings that looked as though they had been chosen many years before, and they weren't at all to her taste. She sighed and decided to look out the window again, losing herself in the snow-covered garden. She felt very thankful the holiday season was already upon them and hoped it would bring all of them together as a family.

"Rebecca, have you had any luck finding the book of fairy tales now that our things have arrived?" asked Lady Tremaine.

"Not yet, my lady. I'll be sure to give it to you the moment I find it," Rebecca said as Nanny Pinch came into the room with Anastasia and Drizella.

"Ah, my lovely girls," Lady Tremaine said, reaching out her arms so they could come in for hugs. "How are you, my darlings? I presume Nanny Pinch is helping you get settled in your new rooms?"

"Yes, Mama, but we hate it here. Cinderella is

rude, the house is empty, and we hate Sir Richard!" said Anastasia.

"It's true, Mama, we hate it. We thought you were bringing us to a magical place, not some old stone house in the middle of nowhere. We can't even see the castle from here," added Drizella.

Cinderella came into the room just then, in time to hear Drizella's complaint.

"That's not true, Drizella, you can see a view of the castle from the attic tower."

Drizella just scoffed in response.

"Now, now, Drizella, be sweet to your new sister," said Lady Tremaine.

"She's not our sister!" said Anastasia.

Nanny Pinch was about to scold both of the girls when Lady Tremaine did her best to create a diversion to appease all of them.

"Nanny Pinch, would you mind serving the tea for the girls in here? And some coffee for me. I would love to just sit and visit with my girls," she said, smiling at Cinderella. "Now, girls, let's acquaint ourselves better while we wait for our tea, shall we? Sit down, Cinderella. We would love to know more about you," she said, motioning for Cinderella to come sit near her, Anastasia, and Drizella. Cinderella took the seat across from them instead, keeping a bit of distance.

"I hope you're enjoying my mother's home, Lady Tremaine," she said, smiling at her stepmother.

Nanny Pinch nearly unsettled the tea cart, she was so shocked by Cinderella's words. "Cinderella, dear, we already talked this over," she said. "This house now belongs to your papa and new mama."

Cinderella just smiled sweetly. "No, Miss Pinch, Papa told me that this house will always be Mama's no matter who calls herself lady of the house."

Lady Tremaine understood what the little girl was saying, even though it stung. She wasn't being malicious, or even trying to be hurtful. She didn't think the girl was even capable of being mean. She was just repeating what her father had told her. The girl simply didn't understand that it hurt her feelings, or why.

"Yes, my dear Cinderella, in a way this house

will always be your mother's because her spirit is kept alive by the memories you have of her here. I think that is a beautiful sentiment." Lady Tremaine reached her hand out for Cinderella to take. "I know I said this already, but it really would please me if you could find it in your heart to call me Mama."

Cinderella was fussing with something in the pocket at the front of her skirts, not paying attention to what Lady Tremaine was saying.

"Cinderella, did you hear your new mama?" asked Nanny Pinch, trying to divert the girl's attention from whatever it was that she was messing with in her pocket. "Cinderella?" she said again.

The girl finally looked up. "Yes?"

"Your new mama was speaking to you."

Cinderella clasped her hands together like a little angel and smiled at Lady Tremaine. "Yes, Lady Tremaine?" she asked.

"Never mind, Cinderella." Lady Tremaine was hurt and exhausted by the entire ordeal. But then Anastasia spoke up. "You're being rude, Cinderella."

"Yes," Drizella chimed in. "Cinderella, why won't you call her Mama?"

Both girls watched as Cinderella ignored them, fiddling with her pocket again.

Lady Tremaine reached for her brooch, running her fingers lightly against the cold jade. She was having a hard time with this young girl already and doing her best to keep patient, but she knew that if one of her own daughters was acting this way she wouldn't stand for it, so she decided she must say something.

"Cinderella, show us what's in your pocket that has you so distracted you can't be bothered to listen to a word my daughters and I have said."

"Oh, I don't think that is a good idea," said Cinderella without looking up.

"Cinderella, show us what's in your pockets now, or I will have Nanny Pinch take you up to your room without any tea," Lady Tremaine scolded, trying to use the same tactics she'd used on her own daughters in the past.

"That's fine. I'd prefer to be in my room right

now anyway, Stepmother," Cinderella said with a smile.

Impossible girl! Lady Tremaine thought. She didn't understand this girl at all. It didn't seem like she was trying to be insolent or hurtful; she was simply stating her truth.

"Very well, Cinderella, go back to your room, but I must insist you call me Mama."

Cinderella walked over to Lady Tremaine, reaching her hand out for her to take. "I'm sorry, Lady Tremaine. I can't call someone who isn't my mother Mama. But I will happily call you Stepmother, if that pleases you." She looked up at Lady Tremaine hopefully.

"Very well, Cinderella." Lady Tremaine sighed, eyeing her strange new stepdaughter warily. "You may stay down here and have your tea with me and your stepsisters before you go back up to your room."

"If that will make you happy, Stepmother," she said, looking back down at her pocket.

"Won't you show us what's in your pocket?" asked Drizella, breaking ranks and joining Cinderella on the love seat.

"Yes, Cinderella, what is it?" asked Anastasia.

"Girls, Nanny Pinch is about to serve. Must you interrogate Cinderella about what's inside her pocket while we drink our tea?" Lady Tremaine said jokingly.

She was very happy to see them getting along a little better, munching on finger sandwiches that Nanny Pinch had made, and sipping their tea like perfect princesses. They had gotten off to a sticky start, but she was at last feeling like they could be a happy family together.

Just then Rebecca came into the room. "The Grand Duke is here, my lady. He says he has a message for you from the castle."

Lady Tremaine stood up, motioning for the girls to do the same. "Show him in," she said.

The tall man walked in, squinting, Lady Tremaine thought, in order to keep his monocle in place. He was a strange man, this duke. But then, Lady Tremaine thought everyone she met here so far was very odd.

"Sorry to disturb you, Lady Tremaine. But our king has sent me to inform you that Sir Richard will be detained for the next several weeks on court business."

Lady Tremaine was starting to get agitated. "On our wedding night, of all nights?" She heard the edge in her voice and stopped herself from going on.

"I'm afraid it's unavoidable, Lady Tremaine. Sir Richard would rather be here, I am sure. But when a king calls one of his knights to his side, it is his duty to the king and the realm to follow orders, no matter what."

Lady Tremaine sighed. "And what exactly will my husband be doing these next few weeks, may I ask?" Lady Tremaine was finding it hard to hide her frustration.

"You may ask, my lady, but I'm afraid I may not answer. Now if you will excuse me, I will be on my way. Welcome to the Many Kingdoms. I'm sure I will be seeing you at court." He bowed curtly and left the room without further ceremony.

Lady Tremaine sat there at a complete loss. This was the most unusual day. She wanted to rant and scream, to cry and vent, but she couldn't. She was in a strange land, in a strange home where she didn't feel welcome, and now her husband—who had only become so a few short hours ago—was mysteriously away on their wedding night without so much as an explanation. And for all she knew he wasn't even the man he presented himself to be when he was in England. She could only hope his coldness to her today after the ceremony was due to stress over this business at the castle, whatever that may be.

"I'm sorry, Cinderella, but it seems your papa will be away for some weeks. I hope your new sisters and I will prove to be a delightful diversion while we await his return," she said, trying to keep her face emotionless.

"Oh, I knew Papa was planning to go away after the wedding," said Cinderella. "He told me." She fiddled again with the thing in her pocket.

"What do you mean he told you?" asked Lady Tremaine with more sharpness in her voice than she intended.

"Papa tells me everything," she said, smiling at whatever it was that had her so preoccupied. Lady

Tremaine was being pushed beyond her limits. She felt the anger rising in her. Sir Richard told his daughter he was going away right after the ceremony? Clearly he had urged her to come here so quickly because he had wanted someone to watch over his daughter for free. The indignities of this day kept mounting and she feared this was just the start.

She got up from her seat and faced the window, staring out at the courtyard and trying to center herself, but then the screaming started, which pierced her ears. Screams so loud she thought her daughters were being murdered. When she turned around, she saw Anastasia and Drizella standing up on the furniture, squealing louder than she thought was possible, while Cinderella frantically searched for something on the floor.

"It's a mouse! A mouse!" said Anastasia.

"Mama! She had a mouse in her pocket and it escaped!" cried Drizella.

"Be quiet, you're going to frighten him," said Cinderella.

"Frighten him?" screamed Drizella.

"It's just a little mouse. See?" Cinderella scooped the little creature up in her hands and held it up very close to Drizella's face. Drizella and Anastasia leaped from their chairs and back to their mother.

"Mama, make her take that horrible thing away!" said Drizella.

Lady Tremaine stroked her brooch, trying to find a calm, cool place in her heart so she could handle this matter without getting too angry with her new stepdaughter.

"Girls, girls, please calm down. Now, Cinderella, we can't have you keeping mice in your pocket. They're dirty creatures. Get rid of it immediately."

Cinderella looked confused. "Excuse me, Stepmother, but they aren't dirty. Look, I've even made him something to wear." She held up the mouse for her stepmother so she could see the trembling creature's smart little pair of green trousers, his dandy red shirt, and jaunty cap.

"Cinderella! Get that thing out of my face this instant! That all very well may be, but I won't have you keeping mice in this house, clothed or not.

They're foul, dirty, diseased things! I must insist you take that mouse outside and let it free."

For the first time, Cinderella looked insolent and was purposely defying her stepmother. "I won't! The mice are mine and I refuse to let them go. A cat might get him if I put him outside."

Lady Tremaine willed herself not to slap the girl. "Mice? Are you telling me there is more than this one? Cinderella, I demand you release them all into the garden."

"No!" she said, putting the frightened mouse back into her pocket and stomping her foot.

"Cinderella! Do as I say! Take that mouse out of your pocket immediately! It's going to make you sick."

Cinderella shook her head. "I don't know what mice are like in London, but they are nothing but safe and friendly in the Many Kingdoms. Now if you'll excuse me . . ." she said, turning to leave.

"Cinderella! Don't you dare walk away from me—"

And just then the mouse jumped out of Cinderella's pocket and bolted toward Lady Tremaine and her daughters, who jumped back onto the chairs, screaming again.

"Girls! Please calm down! Cinderella, come back here this moment!" Lady Tremaine looked up to see Cinderella leaving the room, and even though she couldn't see her face, she thought for sure that she was smiling.

"Come on, little one, we mustn't stay where we're not wanted," said Cinderella as she left the room. The mouse scampered along behind her.

After Cinderella left, Lady Tremaine needed Nanny Pinch's help to calm down Drizella and Anastasia. When they were sitting quietly again and sipping tea, Lady Tremaine took a deep breath.

"What an appalling girl!" she said, immediately regretting saying so in front of her own daughters. Then Rebecca cleared her throat.

"Yes, Rebecca?"

"I didn't want to say so in front of Cinderella, my

lady, but it's true that mice in the Many Kingdoms are entirely safe. They don't carry disease like they do in London." She winced as she spoke and clearly felt bad about the entire ordeal.

"Nevertheless, find me a cat," said Lady Tremaine, narrowing her eyes and touching her brooch. "Come on, girls. Let's go to our rooms and rest. Tomorrow morning we will go into the village to hire servants and buy things we need for the house. Nanny Pinch can stay here with Cinderella. Rebecca, you will come with us. You can show us around the village, and while you do so you can impart your wisdom about this strange place we now call home."

CHAPTER XII

THE LITTLE DEVIL

It had been several weeks since Sir Richard had left for the palace when Lady Tremaine received word that his mysterious court business was at an end and he would be returning home that evening. She had decided that she was really quite happy he had been away. It had given her a chance to get their house in order, buy all new furniture, hire servants, and smooth things over as much as she could with Cinderella. She hadn't completely shaken the hurt from their rocky first day together, but she hoped things would be better once Sir Richard was home.

She was sad to see Nanny Pinch go back to London, but she had hired a wonderful governess for all the girls by the name of Nanny. Lady Tremaine had asked her if she'd like to go by her actual name accompanied by the title Nanny, but it seemed Nanny was her actual name. So Nanny it was.

She was a lovely older lady with white hair and sparkling eyes. She was a dream of a nanny, patient and kind, and worked wonders with all the girls. They spent their days in the schoolroom, or picnicking in the garden. She encouraged them to put on plays in the library and took them to the village for tea so they could practice being proper young ladies.

Lady Tremaine was quite frankly happy to have the girls out of her hair while she got the house in order and ready for her husband's return. Since Nanny and the other servants were hired, life felt more like it had back in London. She didn't constantly have the girls under her feet, and she was feeling less alone. Life was running perfectly again.

As the hour approached for her husband's return,

she became nervous. She went from room to room checking to see if the house was flawless, following behind the maids to make sure everything was just so. She was sure there were flowers in every room, and their home was pristinely clean.

As she did her rounds for the fourth or fifth time, fussing again in her bedroom making sure everything was just right, Rebecca came into the room holding a small basket and wearing a wide grin.

"What do you have there, Rebecca, and why do you look so pleased with yourself?" Lady Tremaine asked.

"It's a gift for you," Rebecca said, handing her the basket. "To make up for leaving behind the book of fairy tales." She looked as though she felt truly sorry, and seemed to have been brooding about it since she had unpacked Lady Tremaine's things to find she hadn't packed it after all.

"Perhaps it wasn't left behind, Rebecca. Don't rebuke yourself too much. I am sad not to have it, but maybe it will turn up." Lady Tremaine looked in the basket and noticed there was something wiggling under some red silk.

"You didn't!" Lady Tremaine squealed like a little girl. She lifted the red silk to reveal the sweetest little black-and-white kitten she had ever seen. "You did! Oh, Rebecca, he is precious." She took him out of the basket and held him up to get a better look at his adorable face. "Oh my goodness. Who are you? And look at his smart bow!" He squirmed in her hands, and she placed him on the bed. "He is so cute, Rebecca, thank you."

Just then the kitten sprang off the bed, attaching himself to Lady Tremaine's beautiful dress and making her laugh. "Oh, you little devil!" she said, detaching the kitten from her dress. "I think I will name you Lucifer. That's the perfect name for a devilish creature like you, ruining my beautiful dress."

"Here, my lady, let me take him for you." Rebecca gingerly took the kitten from Lady Tremaine and put him back in the basket. "I will keep him for you this evening. You don't need . . . what did you say his name was again?" she asked.

"Lucifer," said Lady Tremaine. Rebecca still looked puzzled so Lady Tremaine explained. "He's a devil, the ruler of the underworld."

Recognition dawned on her face. "Oh, like Hades!" she said, laughing. "Yes, this little guy is mischievous. I think the name fits." She smiled and gave him a pat on the head. "It doesn't look like he damaged your dress," she said, squinting at it closely, and then looking up at Lady Tremaine's face. "You look beautiful, my lady. I'm sure Sir Richard will swoon."

Lady Tremaine wasn't so sure but didn't say so to Rebecca.

"Oh," Rebecca added, "my lady, you've forgotten your favorite brooch." She went to the vanity to fetch it for her.

"I don't feel like wearing it this evening," said Lady Tremaine. It reminded her of her late husband, and tonight she wanted to focus on the future.

"I assume you've been down to the kitchen a few times to make sure the cook has everything in hand?" asked Rebecca.

"Yes. I think she would have chased me out with a broom if she thought she could get away with it," Lady Tremaine said, making Rebecca laugh again.

"I checked in on the girls before I came up," Rebecca continued. "I told Nanny I wanted them to have their dinner and baths early this evening. I thought it would be nice to have the girls in bed right after dinner so you and Sir Richard can enjoy the rest of your evening together alone."

Lady Tremaine wondered if that was a good idea. "Cinderella will want to see her father," she said. "Tell Nanny Sir Richard and I will come in to kiss the girls before they go to sleep, don't you think?"

"That's a lovely idea," Rebecca agreed, sighing. "Oh, my lady, you have such a wonderful evening planned. Cook is making all of Sir Richard's favorites for dinner, and I'll make sure everything is ready for you in here while you two are having dinner. That way it's a surprise."

Lady Tremaine was getting more nervous by the moment. She was hoping with all her heart the man returning to her from the castle was the man she had met in London and not the one who dashed away right after their wedding. "Thank you, Rebecca dear. This is going to be an evening to remember."

⚜ ⚜ ⚜ ⚜

Lady Tremaine assembled the entire staff to greet her husband upon his return. She thought it would be a lovely surprise for him to see how well she had staffed their home while he had been away. They were all lined up in the vestibule in their smart black-and-white uniforms, positioned on either side of the entryway to leave a pathway for Sir Richard so he could walk through and greet each one.

Lady Tremaine stood in the center of the assembly right up front so she could greet her husband the moment he walked through the door. Anastasia, Drizella, and Cinderella stood at the foot of the grand staircase in their prettiest dresses. They looked as perfect as a portrait, all of them standing still and ladylike.

They were all startled by the front door flying open without ceremony, Sir Richard's voice booming.

"Hello, my love, my most beautiful girl," he said, walking toward Lady Tremaine. She felt foolish for dreading this moment, worrying if he loved her, wondering if he would be happy to see her when he got home.

"Welcome home, my love," she said, ready to receive his embrace, but he didn't take her into his arms. Instead, he passed right by her, rushing over to Cinderella, who was waiting for him, tears in her eyes.

"My sweet girl! How are you? Did you miss your papa?"

Lady Tremaine had never seen a man so happy to see his daughter. He hugged her so tightly she thought he might crush the poor girl.

Lady Tremaine put her hand to her chest to

feel for her favorite brooch, but it wasn't there. She needed it. She needed that extra layer, something to protect her heart. She stood there feeling exposed, hurt and lost, but she found her composure and walked down the length of her servants, all of whom were giving her sad looks, to join her husband and daughters.

"I did miss you, Papa! I don't have to go to bed already, do I? Nanny says that Stepmother says we do, but I want to stay up and hear about your adventures. And I don't have to get rid of my mice, do I?" she said, wrapping her arms around his neck.

He laughed. "Of course you don't have to go to bed early or get rid of your mice, my angel. And who is this Nanny?" He looked up then, finally noticing the assembled staff.

"Excuse me a moment, my beautiful girl, I have neglected to say hello to your stepsisters and stepmother. Anastasia, Drizella," he said, looking at them. "And my lady. May I speak with you in the other room?"

Lady Tremaine flinched. She wasn't sure what to expect. Did he want to be alone with her because he didn't feel comfortable showing affection in front of the servants? From the tone of his voice it sounded like she was in for a scolding, though she couldn't fathom what would warrant it.

"Of course, my husband," she said, narrowing her eyes at him while she followed him into his study.

He took a seat behind his large antique desk, leaving her standing like she was a petulant schoolgirl about to be reprimanded by her headmaster. "What is the meaning of this? Explain yourself."

She blinked a few times, trying to figure out what he meant. "Are you talking about the mice? I told her I'm sorry, Richard. I didn't realize they weren't like London mice."

Sir Richard shook his head as if shaking off a bad thought. "Of course our mice are different from London mice! Did you say she couldn't have her mice? You're not to deny Cinderella anything she wants, do you understand? She's lost her mother."

Lady Tremaine stayed silent. She understood his sentiment. She had felt the same way after her husband died.

"I'm not talking about the blasted mice anyway. What is the meaning of all these new things and hiring all this staff? Did I say you could do that?" he asked.

She reached again for her brooch, feeling like she needed it. "I didn't think I required your permission," she said, finding her courage and her voice.

"Well, you do."

She didn't understand why she was holding her tongue. She never would have with Lord Tremaine. Perhaps it was simply that she couldn't believe this was their first real conversation after they were married. Perhaps it was that she didn't want to start off his return on the wrong foot, like she had with Cinderella. "I know you're used to being independent, spending your money as you will, but your overindulgence and extravagance have no place here, my lady. Your rank means nothing in the Many Kingdoms. I am the lord of this domain."

Lady Tremaine shook her head. "If it's a matter of expense, Sir Richard, let me assure you that the money I spent was entirely mine."

Sir Richard scoffed. "No, the money is mine. We are married now. And I will dictate how it's spent." He continued, "To that end, where are all my wife's tasteful things that you have so thoughtlessly replaced with all this garish rubbish?"

Lady Tremaine lowered her eyes. She felt horrible. She didn't think replacing their old things would upset him so much. It hadn't occurred to her that all the shabby furnishings held meaning.

"I'm sorry, Sir Richard. I donated them," she said.

He slammed his fist on his desk. "I'm not sure I can forgive this. You have really overstepped." He looked up at the portrait of his wife hanging over the fireplace, and his face softened. He looked sad, almost resigned. "Well, there is nothing to be done about it now," he said, "but you will let the staff go first thing tomorrow."

"And who will clean the house, make the meals, and care for the children?" she asked, willing herself not to cry before him. She reached for her brooch again and was again disappointed not to find herself wearing it.

"You will," he said. "Now if you'll excuse me, I want to spend some time with my daughter."

CHAPTER XIII

CHRISTMAS EVE

Lady Tremaine let most of the staff go as her husband had demanded, except for Nanny and Rebecca, whom he reluctantly agreed to let stay on. She had lost everything. Her home in London, all her money, and her dignity now belonged to him. She had written to her old solicitor at the behest of Lady Hackle, but there was nothing Lady Tremaine could do about her circumstances. All her money was now her husband's, as was the law in the Many Kingdoms: upon marriage all assets are controlled by the woman's husband or father, unless both are deceased. Lady Tremaine had known this going into the marriage. It wasn't, after all, very different from how things worked in London, and she hadn't been worried about it at the time. Based on his rank, she had assumed Sir Richard had more money than she did. But she soon found out she couldn't have been more wrong.

Her solicitor had done some investigating and found that before his marriage to Lady Tremaine, Sir Richard had been penniless and in desperate need to marry a lady of means to keep his estate. He had been in considerable debt to the Crown and used the majority of Lady Tremaine's fortune to pay it off. She understood now why he was so furious she had hired such a large staff and assumed that his debt was the "court business" he had rushed off to sort out, though as far as she was concerned it didn't account for the amount of time he was away. She had asked him several times what he had done while he was at the castle, but he had skirted the subject, saying it was a matter for men and that she should stay in her place as lady of the house.

She soon found herself miserable, alone, and depressed. She collapsed on her bed at the end of each day, too tired to even spend time with her girls. Frankly, she was ashamed to have them see her in such a state. Her only companion was her kitten, Lucifer, who was always at her side—that is, when he wasn't hunting the mice that Cinderella tried to bring into her foul menagerie. There was nothing she could do about the mice Cinderella already kept, Sir Richard made that abundantly clear, but she was determined to keep the girl from acquiring more.

Lady Tremaine's days were spent cleaning the entire house, scrubbing its floors, dusting, beating the rugs, doing the dishes, making the meals, polishing the silver, replacing the candles in all the sconces and chandeliers, lighting the fires, doing the laundry, and more—all under the watchful eye of Sir Richard's first wife. She surveyed everything Lady Tremaine did from the portraits of her that hung in almost every room of the château. And Cinderella was always there to remind her that the house was still her mother's, to complain that she missed their old furnishings or the way her mother used to keep things. Lady Tremaine felt unwelcome. She had become a servant in her own home. Thank goodness for Nanny, who saw to the girls, and for Rebecca, who did her best to help Lady Tremaine as well as she could.

Before long it was Christmas Eve, and Lady Tremaine wanted to make an evening of it. She and her girls were entitled to a bit of celebration. Rebecca was preparing a lavish meal for the family at her request. Lady Tremaine wasn't able to buy gifts for the girls, but she had a few things of her own that she thought they would appreciate, so she had wrapped them up. She planned to put them under the tree, which Nanny had so thoughtfully agreed to decorate while the girls were napping.

Nanny had arranged a special project for the girls that week, helping them to make silver stars and golden moons out of paper, without telling them they would be used to decorate the tree. She and Lady Tremaine thought it would be a lovely surprise for the girls to see their creations displayed so prominently on the family tree. It would be one more way they all could celebrate together.

Lady Tremaine was exhausted from this long day. She had gotten up early to finish all her housework. Without the assistance of Rebecca and Nanny, she wouldn't have had time to make herself presentable for dinner, or to arrange the gifts that she was so excited to give the girls. She just wished her husband would agree to let her hire some more staff. She hated adding to Nanny's and Rebecca's duties when they already had so much work of their own to do.

As she was passing Sir Richard's study, she decided she would ask him if they couldn't hire someone, at least in the kitchen. As it was she had been prevailing upon Rebecca too often with special meals, even though it wasn't her job.

As she stood in front of his study door, she willed herself to have the courage to go in, trying to evoke something of her old self, but she felt ugly, covered in the soot she had been scrubbing off the floors. As she reached for the knob she saw her raw, cracked, and swollen hands. She sighed, deciding it would be better to bring this matter up with her husband later after he'd had the special dinner she planned.

Lady Tremaine had decided to wear the red dress she had worn the evening Sir Richard proposed to her, and she asked Nanny to see that the girls were also dressed festively, making sure to remind her to check Cinderella's pockets for mice before she came down to the dining room.

The dining room looked lovely. Lady Tremaine had decorated the mantel, windows, and doorways with holly and filled the room with white candles. She had stockings by the fireplace, one for each of the three girls, with little things she had made for them and trinkets of her own she thought they would enjoy. She had even made a little outfit for one of Cinderella's mice out of one of her old sparkly handbags. And the tree was magnificent, glistening in the candlelight, showcasing the girls' decorations. It was going to be the perfect evening.

As she stood in the dining room entryway waiting for the girls and Sir Richard, she felt like her old self again. She reached up and touched her jade brooch, which she had made sure to pin to the bodice of her dress tonight. She loved how cold the stone felt beneath her fingers and thought that was how she would like to feel: cold, strong, and solid. Nothing Sir Richard could say to her this evening would sway her or knock her down. She felt sturdy and unmovable, like a statue.

And then she saw them, her girls, coming down the staircase in their vibrant red velvet Christmas dresses. Cinderella was in gold, and all of them looked like beautiful Christmas angels.

Sir Richard came down a few minutes later, narrowing his eyes at the festive dresses and decorations. "And what's this?" he said as he got closer. "Well, don't you look beautiful, Cinderella." He smiled down at his daughter. "What's the occasion?" he asked, looking at Lady Tremaine, Anastasia, and Drizella. "Why are you dressed in red?" He glanced into the dining room. "And what's that?"

"Oh, Mama, you remembered," said Anastasia, hugging her mother.

"It's Christmas Eve!" Drizella clapped her hands together with glee.

"What is the meaning of this? Explain yourself," Sir Richard said, taking in the stockings hanging over the fireplace.

"Those are Christmas stockings, my husband."

Anastasia and Drizella dashed over to peek at what was inside. "You know the rules, girls, no peeking. You may open your gifts after we have had dinner if you like," Lady Tremaine said, laughing. "Cinderella, there is a stocking for you, too."

"Thank you, Stepmother," she said carefully, eyeing her father.

Sir Richard's face was red. "Have this tree taken down at once!" he said, his voice low and angry.

"Oh, Papa, she didn't know," said Cinderella, trying to calm her father down. "Look, Anastasia, Drizella, and I made these decorations ourselves!"

Sir Richard frowned at her. "You knew about this and didn't tell me?"

Cinderella took her father's hand. "I didn't know why we were making the decorations, Father. I'm sorry. But isn't the tree lovely? I missed having one for the solstice, and it was so thoughtful of Lady Tremaine to do all this for us," she said, which surprised Lady Tremaine. It made her like the girl a bit more.

Sir Richard walked away from his daughter, standing in front of the fireplace looking at the portrait of his wife. She looked just like Cinderella but older. It was as if he were having a conversation with her in his mind, reconciling something with her.

Anastasia, Drizella, and Lady Tremaine just stood there watching, not knowing what to do.

"What did I do wrong, Cinderella? Why is your father so upset?" Lady Tremaine whispered.

"The solstice was a special time for Mama and Papa. That is when he proposed. We always made a grand party of it."

Lady Tremaine understood. "I'm sorry, Richard. I didn't know. Can't we start a tradition of our own and celebrate Christmas? If not for us, then for the girls?"

He turned around with a sneer. "And this is how you celebrate in London, by hanging laundry on the fireplace mantel? It's a mockery of the solstice," he said, shaking his head.

"But I've arranged a Christmas dinner for all of us. Rebecca has been preparing it all day." She held her breath, hoping he wouldn't disappoint the girls.

"We don't celebrate Christmas in the Many Kingdoms. Rebecca should have told you that," he said angrily.

"Papa, won't you please just sit down and enjoy the dinner Stepmother has arranged? We could have a lovely evening, Papa, if you just try." Cinderella went to her father and gave him a kiss. "Please, Papa. For me?"

To Lady Tremaine's surprise, his face softened. "Very well, my angel, you know I can't deny you," he said, and motioned for everyone to sit down to dinner.

Dinner went well enough, all things considered. Rebecca had made them a feast, though Lady Tremaine was wondering why she and Nanny had neglected to tell her that Christmas wasn't celebrated in the Many Kingdoms. Sir Richard's words still stung, but it was enlightening to see where some of his harshness had come from. She and her girls sat quietly through most of dinner as Sir Richard lavished most of his attention on his daughter, who was trying her best to bring everyone into the conversation.

"Isn't this a wonderful dinner, Papa? Lady Tremaine did a wonderful job, don't you think?" she said, surprising Lady Tremaine even more. She wondered if she and Cinderella might after all become friends.

"I understand Rebecca made the meal," he said, shoveling more food into his mouth greedily. It made Lady Tremaine slightly queasy. She detested poor manners at the dinner table. She detested most things about Sir Richard, she had found. She sat there looking at him with disgust, wondering how she ever fell for his skullduggerous ways. She had thought he was so charming when they first met, and now she could hardly hide her contempt for him.

"Yes, she is a very good cook." Lady Tremaine smiled at Cinderella to let her know she appreciated her trying to lighten the mood at the table.

"Though that isn't Rebecca's job, is it? The lady of the house should make the meals," he said.

"I dare say the court has a cook, and so do half the people of this village," said Lady Tremaine. "I don't see why we can't hire one and a couple of girls to help around the house. It's really too much for me to manage on my own."

Sir Richard laughed. "Are you comparing yourself with the queen now? Are you so high and mighty you can't cook for your family?"

Lady Tremaine ran her fingers across her brooch. "Of course not, husband. But it wouldn't hurt to get some help around this house, and I must insist that we do." She felt brave sitting there before him, wearing the brooch her previous husband had given her. She felt strong, and there was nothing he could do to make her feel otherwise. Or at least that is how she felt in that moment.

"Well, if it means that much to you, then yes. You can have some help," he said, pushing his plate away from him now that he was finished, another habit she detested. "But you won't need to hire anyone. The girls can help you." He patted his stomach like a fat king.

"But what of their education? I thought you agreed that Stasia, Zella, and Cinderella would continue their studies," said Lady Tremaine.

"Oh, Cinderella will continue her education. I meant your girls. Anastasia and Drizella," he said.

Anastasia and Drizella leaped up from their seats.

"What does he mean, Mama?" asked Drizella, running over to her mother.

Anastasia was close behind. "He can't be serious!"

"That isn't fair," said Cinderella. It shocked Lady

Tremaine that Cinderella was standing up for her stepsisters.

"You are such a dear girl, Cinderella, and you're turning into a beautiful young woman, just like your mother. It's remarkable how much you favor her," he said, ignoring Anastasia and Drizella and smiling at his daughter. "I think it's time to present you to court. I have long held a wish that you and the prince would eventually marry."

Cinderella dropped her fork, which fell to her plate with a loud clank. "Oh, Papa, I will never leave you. Not ever," she said.

"Well, I think it's a wonderful idea to present the girls to court," said Lady Tremaine, eagerly scanning his face to guess what he might be thinking before he replied. But his answer was quite clear.

"I don't intend to present your girls to court, Lady Tremaine. They will be far too busy in the kitchen helping you."

Lady Tremaine was livid. "I wonder that you didn't just hire a housekeeper, Sir Richard, because it's clear that is all you wanted from the start," said Lady Tremaine.

Sir Richard scoffed. "Housekeepers don't come with large dowries, and besides, I'd have to pay a housekeeper," he said, sneering at her.

Chapter XIV

The Odd Sisters

Five long years passed since that horrible Christmas Eve, and the girls were now old enough to be presented at court, but Sir Richard wouldn't hear of it.

"But why won't you let my girls be presented along with Cinderella?" Lady Tremaine had broached the subject as he was heading out the door on castle business one morning.

"I don't have time for this conversation again. Standards are different in the Many Kingdoms. Your girls are just not, well, very presentable, shall we say, and I would be ashamed to claim them as my own in public. I'm sure you understand." He tried to put an end to the conversation by scurrying out the door, but Lady Tremaine followed him.

"I do not understand! What are you saying? My girls are beautiful!" she said sincerely, for she truly felt that way. But Sir Richard laughed.

"You really believe that, don't you?" he said, making his way to the carriage. "I must leave now, I'm late. And I won't hear any more of this, do you understand?"

The carriage drove off, leaving Lady Tremaine standing there. She was livid, but there was nothing she could do. She was trapped in the Many Kingdoms, trapped in that house, and trapped in a marriage. Her only hope was to try writing to Lady Hackle again. Lady Tremaine and her daughters couldn't stay any longer. They were in misery. She had written to her friend Lady Hackle quite some time back to see if she could send her the money so she and her daughters could book passage back to London, but she never replied, which had begun to concern Lady Tremaine because she hadn't heard from her friend since soon after she had arrived in the Many Kingdoms. She had been hoping once the girls were of age they could marry the Hackle boys and they, at least, would be free from this wretched place, but with no word from Lady Hackle she was starting to worry that she and her daughters would find no escape from Sir Richard or the Many Kingdoms.

She went to her room to compose another letter and found her daughters crying on her bed. "Oh, my girls, what's the matter?" she asked, rushing to put her arms around them.

"We heard what Sir Richard said. He thinks we are ugly," said Drizella.

"No one will ever want to marry us," said Anastasia.

"That's not true, my doves. You're both beautiful. And don't forget you're betrothed to the Hackle boys. In fact, I was just about to write Lady Hackle to see if you could go there for a visit."

The girls' faces brightened.

"Really, Mama? Won't you come with us?" said Anastasia. "We know how unhappy you are. Why not just leave this place? Sir Richard is horrible. We never go anywhere or do anything. We're always trapped inside doing housework, and no one ever comes to visit us. We hate it here!"

"I hate it here, too, my darlings. And if you can keep a secret, I'll tell you what I really plan to do. I've been writing Lady Prudence asking if she can send us money to book passage to London as soon as possible. I promise I won't keep you here a moment longer than I can help. I will do anything to get you out of this house. Mark my words." She hugged them tight.

"Thank you, Mama," said Drizella.

"Very well, my dears, off with you to take your lessons with Nanny while Sir Richard is at the castle. I will do your chores; he needn't know you didn't do them. Go now and learn as much as you can while he is away and let me write my letter to Lady Prudence." She kissed them both before they dashed out of the room.

As she was writing her letter, Rebecca came into

the room. "Excuse me, my lady, I was looking for Lucifer. Cinderella says he's been menacing her mice again, and I wanted to have a chat with him."

"Try the kitchen, he likes teasing the dog. Or maybe up in the attic; he loves how warm it is up there, because it gets lots of sun." Lady Tremaine didn't look up from writing her letter.

"I can take that letter to the village to be sent off to Lady Hackle once you are finished," Rebecca offered. Lady Tremaine raised her eyebrow. "By the way, did Lady Hackle ever say if she found the book of fairy tales? I feel just awful I didn't find it in any of the trunks."

"She didn't. I will include a postscript inquiring again," she said, signing the letter and putting it into an envelope. As she wrote out the address and affixed her wax seal, she wondered how Rebecca knew she was writing to Lady Hackle. Then again, who else in all the world would she be writing to?

"Before you go, please tell Nanny to keep an

eye out for Sir Richard's return. I wouldn't like him to find Anastasia and Drizella taking lessons with Cinderella," she said.

"I understand, my lady." Rebecca took the letter from Lady Tremaine and left.

Finally alone, Lady Tremaine let out a great sigh. She had decided there was no way she and her daughters could stay another fortnight in that château. If she didn't hear back from Lady Hackle within the week, she would steal back her own money if she had to, and if there was none to be had, then she would sell something. But one way or another she would leave this place.

She looked up and saw a face she didn't recognize in the mirror. It was her own face, of course, but it didn't seem like it belonged to her. She looked old, haggard, and worn-out from all the drudgery of keeping Sir Richard's house—Sir Richard's *first wife's* house, she corrected herself. She could never shake that woman, not with all the portraits around the house haunting her, the eyes watching her every step. At least Cinderella had been sweet to her since that Christmas Eve dinner. It did make things somewhat easier, though they hadn't exactly become friends. How could they, when Lady Tremaine resented her for being treated like a princess while she and her daughters were used like servants and degraded at every opportunity?

It had already been a long day and Lady Tremaine still had all her housework to do, along with her daughters'. This had become the custom on the days Sir Richard was at court, and she was thankful no one in the household had alerted him to her little deception.

As she made her way downstairs to start her day's work she heard a knock at the front door. No one ever came to visit them, and so a sudden thrill washed over her. What if it was the Grand Duke to let her know Sir Richard had been killed? She instantly felt bad for thinking so.

She opened the door and found three identical women standing there. They were young women, but at the same time there was something ancient about them, giving them an odd look of timelessness. They were an indistinguishable trio of witches, with stark white faces and large, deep-set eyes that protruded bulbously from their heavily darkened sockets, which was in morbid contrast to their vividly painted cheeks and lips. Lady Tremaine didn't know what to make of these women and thought perhaps they were traveling actors wishing to put on a display for the family.

"Hello, ladies, may I help you?" she asked, looking them up and down. All three wore voluminous long black dresses cinched tightly at the waist, with bodices trimmed in silver, and sparkly golden flower arrangements in their black hair.

"We are here to help *you*, Lady Tremaine," said the woman in the middle. "My name is Lucinda, and these are my sisters, Ruby and Martha." She motioned to her sisters in succession, with the eeriest smile Lady Tremaine had ever seen. But before Lady Tremaine could speak, Lucinda got the strangest look on her face, and within moments both of her sisters looked as if they were panic-stricken. "My sisters and I sense that you have a servant here by the name of Nanny, is that true? Please tell us you haven't given her your brooch. We don't see you wearing it," she said, trying to peer into the house, her eyes wide like a wild bird.

Lady Tremaine was taken aback. "I don't see how that's any of your business," she said. "And how do you know about my brooch?" She reached for it and was surprised to find it wasn't there, then remembered she always took it off to do the house-cleaning. "Who exactly are you women?" she asked. Something about them made it hard for her to keep her thoughts straight. She kept feeling as if she was trying to bring herself out of a haze after each time they spoke.

"Oh, this is a small kingdom, my lady," said Lucinda, cackling to herself under her breath.

"Yes, very small," said Ruby.

"Your story is well known to us. We're watching it being written," said Martha.

"We know of your hardships, my lady. We know

you're a prisoner in your own home. A servant to Sir Richard and his brat daughter, Cinderella. But we can help," said Lucinda.

"Yes, Lady Tremaine, we can help you," said Ruby, taking a small bottle from her pocket and holding it before Lady Tremaine. "The laws in the Many Kingdoms are similar to those in England. Should your husband die, all the money would revert to you since there is no male heir." She smirked.

Lady Tremaine backed away from the sisters, scared and revolted. What were they suggesting? And what was in that little glass bottle?

Her fear only made them laugh, which made Lady Tremaine's head swim more.

"Oh, don't play the dainty little thing with us, Lady Tremaine. We know your heart. It's what brought us to you. Only moments ago you were wishing for Sir Richard's death," said Lucinda, laughing.

"It's really the only way out of this," said Martha.

"Yes, the only way," Ruby added, joining in her sisters' laughter.

Lady Tremaine had the terrible and sudden

realization that Mrs. Bramble had been right about this place. Could it be that these were the witches she had warned her about? The authors of the book of fairy tales, standing right in front of her?

"I suggest you leave here at once before I call someone to throw you out," said Lady Tremaine.

The sisters laughed again as they pressed their way into the house inch by inch.

"Who are you going to call?" asked Martha, advancing on Lady Tremaine, causing her to back up farther and farther into the house. The two women were practically nose to nose.

"Keep away from me, you witches!" Lady Tremaine stumbled backward as all three witches slowly bore down on her. The odd trio laughed even louder.

"Your lady's maid is off sending a letter to your friend in London that will never reach her hands, and your nanny is so old she has forgotten she is the most powerful witch in the Many Kingdoms, aside from our sister Circe, that is. You are quite literally alone and powerless, Lady Tremaine, but we can help you. Just take this." Martha took Lady Tremaine's hand, put the small glass bottle in it, and closed her fingers over it with a theatrical wink.

"Keep it. Just in case you need it," Ruby said.

Her sister Lucinda added, "And should you ever need us, just call to us from any of your mirrors and we will be here."

But before Lady Tremaine could reply, the witches went flying backward all at once, and the door slammed closed behind them with a powerful blast. Lady Tremaine quickly turned around and saw Nanny standing there.

"What in the heavens just happened, Nanny? Did you . . . How did you do that?" asked Lady Tremaine, clutching at her chest and wishing her brooch was there. She ran to the window and saw the three strange sisters standing a good twenty feet away, dusting off their dresses. "They're still here, Nanny!" She rushed to lock the door.

"Those locks won't help you. Go to your room and bring me your brooch. It's time we give it back to its rightful owners," Nanny said.

But Lady Tremaine didn't comply. "Those women said you would ask me for my brooch. They were trying to help me, encouraging me to wear it." She eyed the old woman warily.

"Of course they're encouraging you to wear it; it's cursed! They know you're too smart to fall for their trickery and manipulations, so the only way to seduce you is through curses," said Nanny, heading up the stairs.

"And just where are you going, witch?" spat Lady Tremaine.

"Upstairs to get your brooch," Nanny said. "That's one thing the sisters weren't lying about. I did come here to retrieve it, but Rebecca was always encouraging you to wear it."

"What does Rebecca have to do with it, and why did those women say my letter would never reach London?" asked Lady Tremaine, trying to wrap her mind around all this.

"I imagine the Odd Sisters are intercepting your correspondences, to keep you under their control. They say they want to help you, yet they lured you here just as it was written in the book of fairy tales. I've always found their ways confusing, honestly. Their good intentions tend to run afoul. Oh, Lady Tremaine, I wish I could tell you more, but I fear I've already overstepped by telling you my purpose. I fear you will just have to trust me when I say it's of paramount importance that I have your brooch." She started to make her way up the first set of stairs, but Lady Tremaine was right behind her and seized her by the arm.

"You will not take my brooch! It was given to me by my first husband, and it's the only thing I have left of him. You and Rebecca are the witches, hiding in my house, plotting against me, making me look the fool in front of Sir Richard. Those women warned me about you. They said you would want to take the brooch!"

Nanny sighed. "It's true," she said. "Those women are the Odd Sisters, and I'm afraid Rebecca has been working with them. I have the strangest feeling she thinks she is helping you, encouraging you to wear the brooch, keeping the book of fairy tales from you, but believe me, Lady Tremaine, every time the Odd Sisters and their ilk try to help someone it turns into a disaster. You have to trust me; I'm not here to harm you, I'm here to help. Haven't I kept your secrets from Sir Richard? Don't I care for your girls and teach them in secret? Does that sound like a person who is plotting against you?"

Lady Tremaine released her grip on Nanny's arm, realizing she had been squeezing it rather hard. "What are you then, if not a witch? Some sort of fairy godmother?" Lady Tremaine asked, making the old woman laugh.

"No, that's my sister. But a fairy godmother is closer to the mark than witch, at least in the way you think of witches anyway," she said, giving Lady Tremaine a kind but sad smile.

Lady Tremaine could see this old woman was telling the truth. She had cared for her daughters for five years and had been nothing but loving and caring to her and her girls since the day she arrived at the château. If only she had known this woman was magical, she would have asked her for help sooner.

"If you're a fairy, then please grant me my wish and free me and my daughters from this horrible place." Lady Tremaine heard her voice crack as she pleaded with Nanny, willing herself not to burst into tears.

Lady Tremaine had never seen so much pity in someone's eyes, not even after her husband had passed away. "Oh my dear, I'm so sorry. I truly wish I could. But I'm simply not allowed to help by using my magic. That's why I have been here, doing what I can without it."

"I don't understand," said Lady Tremaine, throwing her hands up. She was so angry. This place made no sense to her. Maniac witches showing up at her door with a bottle full of poison and fairies pretending to be nannies? "I thought that's what fairies were supposed to do—use magic to help people. Why else would you come here if not to protect me and my daughters? We are in danger! You see how Sir Richard is with us!" Lady Tremaine was desperate, and it seemed only to break Nanny's heart.

"We're not allowed to help villains, my lady, and the book of fairy tales has decreed that's exactly what you're about to become. I physically can't do any magic that would help you."

Lady Tremaine scoffed. "Lies! All of this is lies! Then what may I ask did you just do in the entryway downstairs?"

"I broke the rules. That's what I did, and moments from now I will be summoned back to the Fairylands against my will, and if I don't get that brooch before I go, I fear something terrible will happen. Please listen to me, don't trust those witches. I hope with all my heart you are able to turn this story around and break the curse. Will you please try, Lady Tremaine, try your very best? And I promise I will do what I can with the Fairy Council to talk them into letting me intervene. I'm sure once they realize we fairies have this story all wrong they'll see you're not the villain, but your husband is. Please, Lady Tremaine, I won't be able to help you if you—"

But before Nanny could finish her sentence she disappeared right before Lady Tremaine's eyes.

Lady Tremaine blinked. "Nanny?" she whispered. Lady Tremaine stood there wondering if any of this had actually happened. It wasn't as if she hadn't heard the stories of beasts, witches, fairies, dragons, and giants, but she truly hadn't expected to have any of them in her home, casting spells and refusing to help her. But then again, the Odd Sisters had offered her help, hadn't they? She feared, however, that she couldn't trust them any more than she could trust Nanny or Rebecca. She was utterly alone, and it was up to her to help her daughters out of this horrible place.

CHAPTER XV

THE LETTERS

Lady Tremaine went right to Rebecca's room looking for answers. She felt she didn't have the entire story. She rifled through Rebecca's vanity, her wardrobe, and even under her mattress. She was almost at the point of giving up when she felt one of the floorboards under the rug shift beneath her feet. She might not have even thought twice about it, if she hadn't been searching for something. She pulled back the rug and pushed on the loose floorboard until it popped up, revealing what she had been looking for: a stack of letters all addressed to Lady Hackle. So it was true; Rebecca had never sent the letters. That was why Lady Hackle hadn't responded to a single letter in the last several years. What she didn't expect to find was the book of fairy tales, hidden under the stack of letters. She sat there on the floor thumbing through it, feeling foolish that she hadn't believed Nanny now that she had this proof right in front of her. But then she found a name she recognized. Cinderella.

She began to read her story.

Cinderella

Once upon a time, in a faraway land, there was a tiny kingdom. Peaceful, prosperous, and rich in romance and tradition. Here, in a stately château, there lived a widowed gentleman and his little daughter, Cinderella. Although he was a kind and devoted father and gave his beloved child every luxury and comfort, still he felt she needed a mother's care. And so he married again, choosing for his second wife a woman of good family, with two daughters just Cinderella's age. By name: Anastasia and Drizella. It was upon the untimely death of this good man, however, that the stepmother's true nature was revealed. Cold, cruel, and bitterly jealous of Cinderella's charm and beauty, she was grimly determined to forward the interests of her own two awkward daughters. Thus, as time went by, the château fell into disrepair, for the family fortunes were squandered upon the vain and selfish stepsisters, while Cinderella was abused, humiliated, and finally forced to become a servant in her own house. And yet, through it all, Cinderella remained ever gentle and kind, for with each dawn she found new hope that someday her dreams of happiness would come true.

⚜ ⚜ ⚜ ⚜

Lady Tremaine slammed the book down. "Nonsense, none of this has happened! Sir Richard is alive! And if anyone has squandered our money, it was him," she said, getting angrier. "This is a book of lies. And what if I got my hands on what little money was left and used it to provide for my own daughters? What of it? It's my money!" She was about to throw the book across the room in anger. Instead, she got up and took the book and the stack of letters to her own room, where she put them on her vanity. Then she fastened the brooch to her dress, right over her heart, and paced the room trying to figure out what was going on, trying to wrap her head around everything she learned that day.

She didn't know who to believe or what to think. This book was clearly talking about something that was going to happen in the future, and because of that these fairies—or witches, or whatever they were—thought she was a villain. It didn't make sense.

Just then Sir Richard burst into the room, his face full of wrath. "What is this I hear, that you and your daughters are planning on leaving?"

Lady Tremaine looked up at him in shock, grasping for her brooch and grateful she was wearing it. Nanny had it all wrong. The brooch wasn't cursed. It helped her and gave her strength.

"I don't know what you're talking about, Sir Richard," she said, lying to his face easily. She met his steely gaze.

"Don't lie to me, woman! Cinderella told me that you and your gawky daughters plan to leave the Many Kingdoms. And who do you suppose will care for Cinderella? What kind of woman are you that you could abandon your family?" He came toward her menacingly, and she found herself backing away from him, afraid of what he might do.

"Don't come any closer, I warn you," she said, sure he would strike her.

"And what will you do, oh great and mighty lady?" he asked. "Do you really think you can do anything to me? Or leave the Many Kingdoms, for that matter? You will never leave, I will make sure of it." He slammed the door and locked it behind him.

At the sound of the key turning in the lock, she ran to the door and banged on it, calling out for someone to help her, but to no avail. She was terrified and alone and worried what Sir Richard might do to her daughters. She hated him as she had never hated anyone in her life, but she hated Cinderella even more for telling Sir Richard her secret.

She would never forgive the girl for betraying her.

⚜ ⚜ ⚜ ⚜

Later that evening when Sir Richard unlocked Lady Tremaine's bedroom door, she was standing there waiting for him. In her hand, carefully hidden among the folds of her dress, she clutched the bottle the strange sisters had given her.

Sir Richard barely looked at her, his voice cold.

"Since you seem to have dismissed Nanny and Rebecca, I suppose you'd better get down to the kitchen and make our dinner," he said. Cinderella stood behind him with tears in her eyes.

He continued. "And keep those foolish daughters of yours in line. They've been weeping all evening. I can't bear the sound of it anymore. I don't want to lay eyes on any of you in the dining room. I would like to eat in peace with my daughter. You lot can eat in the kitchen like the help you are." He took Cinderella by the arm and dragged her after him down the hall.

"And where are my girls?" she called after him.

"In the kitchen where they belong," he muttered, not bothering to look back at her.

She stood there for a moment, then remembered what he had said about dismissing Rebecca. But Lady Tremaine *hadn't* dismissed her. Where had she gone? She wondered if those witches had warned her not to come back after Nanny sent them flying out the front door.

Still, something about all this didn't make sense. The only thing she knew for certain was that she and her daughters were trapped with a man she feared would cause her harm. There was only one choice left to her.

Chapter XVI

The Mouse, the Teacup, and the Invitation

After Sir Richard's untimely death things were different in the Tremaine household. The book of fairy tales had gotten some things right. He did die, quite suddenly and all too soon. Lady Tremaine's fortune had been returned to her upon his death, and the story was right that she had squandered it, if you could call trying to care for her children, herself, and a stepdaughter she hated squandering. There wasn't even enough left to book them passage back to England. She was quite literally trapped, with hardly enough money to support her daughters and Cinderella, and she was desperate to do something that could change their circumstances. She tried mailing several letters to Lady Hackle herself, but even without Rebecca's interference, she was almost certain her friend did not receive them. It felt as if the entirety of the Many Kingdoms was conspiring to keep her and her daughters trapped there so they could live out this predestined story.

And just like it was written in the book, one morning as Lady Tremaine was having her coffee in bed, her daughters came screaming into her room. It seemed Cinderella had put a mouse under Anastasia's teacup.

Lady Tremaine had had enough of this mouse nonsense. It was one thing for Cinderella to make clothing for the things when she was a little girl and treat them like living dolls she could play with, but it had become an unhealthy and frankly disturbing obsession now that she was a young lady. She spent all her time up in her room talking to the foul creatures, and Lady Tremaine was starting to become concerned for Cinderella's state of mind.

Nothing ever seemed to faze the girl. She didn't cry at her father's funeral, and she didn't protest when Lady Tremaine insisted she take over the household duties. She even appeared rather pleased when Lady Tremaine told her she would be sleeping in the attic bedroom after her father died. Cinderella simply said, "I understand." It seemed there was nothing Lady Tremaine could do to squash her spirit—the girl even sang as she did her chores.

But the fact was for all Cinderella's smiles and naivety, Lady Tremaine felt the girl had a sinister side. She had been tormenting her daughters since the day they met: she put mice under their teacups, mice in their shoes, mice in their dress pockets, mice in little hats and vests everywhere! Lady Tremaine was sick to death of it. But what she resented most of all was that Cinderella had betrayed her. She had acted so sweet, then turned right around and told her father that she and her daughters were trying to escape. That, Lady Tremaine could never forgive. And now she detested the girl.

And so she found herself once again calling Cinderella into her room to have a talk with her about mice.

"Close the door, Cinderella," she said in a low voice. "Come here." She was stroking her cat, Lucifer, eyes narrowed at the girl. She had been putting up with nonsense like this for years, and she no longer had any patience for it. She had been doing it since day one, and no amount of conversation or punishment helped the matter. Cinderella had never learned, and she would have to accept the consequences.

Of course, Cinderella tried to deny it. But who else would put a mouse *in a matching hat and vest* under a teacup?

"Oh, please, you don't think—" Cinderella tried to defend herself, but Lady Tremaine cut her off.

"Hold your tongue! Now!" she snapped, then continued. "It seems we have time on our hands," she said, picking up her coffee cup and smiling.

"But I was only trying to—" Cinderella began, but again Lady Tremaine cut her off.

"Silence! Time for vicious practical jokes? Perhaps we can put it to better use." She poured cream into her coffee and continued.

"Now . . . let me see. There's the large carpet in the main hall. Clean it! And the windows, upstairs and down. Wash them! Oh, yes . . . and the tapestries, and the draperies . . ." Lady Tremaine felt a sense of power in making Cinderella pay for everything she had done to make her life miserable—the mice, of course, and the unforgivable betrayal. But she also enjoyed it because she and her daughters had spent years cleaning up after Cinderella and doing her father's bidding, all under the watchful eye of her poor, sweet, perfect, deceased mother. The mother Lady Tremaine had never had a hope of replacing. She was delighted to turn the tables now on this deceitful and traitorous little brat. That is how Lady Tremaine saw her. And who could blame her really?

And because she had grown to hate the girl so much, she took delight in not letting her speak.

"But I just fin—"

The fact was, Lady Tremaine hated the sound of Cinderella's simperingly sweet voice. She was sick of it, and she was sick of her. She hated the sight of the girl.

"Do them again!" Lady Tremaine snapped. "And don't forget the garden. Then scrub the terrace . . . sweep the halls . . . and the stairs . . . clean the chimneys. And of course, there's the mending, and the sewing, and the laundry." She took a sip of her coffee. "Oh, yes, and one more thing. See that Lucifer gets his bath," she added, knowing how much Cinderella hated giving Lucifer his bath.

It was mornings like this that gave Lady Tremaine life. They made her feel like the strong, capable woman she was and not the coward she had become under the dominion of Cinderella's father.

However, no amount of tormenting the girl would change their circumstances. She needed a plan. But then a solution to all their problems magically presented itself to her.

An invitation from the castle.

It came that afternoon while she was with her girls, who had been bickering, no doubt because they were feeling high-strung from Cinderella's constant antics.

Lady Tremaine had been under tremendous stress

and agitation but rarely let herself lose control, not since she had started wearing her brooch every day. She held her composure like a statue. Cold, resolute, and in complete control. She did her best to impart this way of thinking to her girls, to no avail. Anastasia and Drizella always had been difficult to control, now that she reflected on it.

The girls became wild as ever when Cinderella brought in the invitation, snatching it back and forth from each other until Lady Tremaine took the letter and read it herself.

"Well, there is to be a ball," she said, realizing this was the perfect opportunity for her girls. If one of them could marry the prince, their prayers would be answered! But then she heard Sir Richard in her mind, laughing at her when she had called her girls beautiful and saying they were not presentable. Of course he thought his own daughter would make a better match for the prince. As much as she believed her daughters were lovely, she couldn't shake the fear that if Cinderella attended the ball with them, Anastasia and Drizella would be overlooked.

Lady Tremaine decided she would do what she could to keep the girl from attending, to give her girls a better chance. The girl had done everything in her power to make Lady Tremaine's life unbearable, and she wasn't going to let the little twit ruin this for her daughters, not after everything she had already done to them. This time her daughters would shine, and they would finally have a happier life, the one she had hoped for when they first moved to this miserable place.

But Cinderella had read the letter herself and pointed out in that too-sweet, simpering voice of hers that the letter said that, by royal decree, every eligible maiden should attend the ball.

"Yes . . . So it does," said Lady Tremaine. "Well, I see no reason why you can't go . . . if you get all your work done."

"Oh, I will! I promise," said Cinderella.

"And if you can find something suitable to wear," she added, knowing full well Cinderella had no ball gowns of her own.

"I'm sure I can! Oh, thank you, Stepmother."

Cinderella left the room smiling, no doubt with visions of marrying the prince dancing in her otherwise feather-filled head.

Lady Tremaine was satisfied. There was no way Cinderella would be able to finish all her housework, make a dress, and still have enough time to get ready for the ball. She touched her brooch happily, thinking about how it would break Cinderella's heart to see them go to the ball without her. But her girls didn't seem to catch on to their mother's plan.

"Mother! Do you realize what you just said?" Drizella asked.

"Of course. I said *if* . . ." said Lady Tremaine, smirking.

CHAPTER XVII

THE BALL

The castle was everything Lady Tremaine had imagined. She felt at home there. It was the first time since she had left England that she felt like she was in familiar surroundings. She was even happy to see the gangly Grand Duke rushing about, though their first uncomfortable meeting years ago had made it impossible to become true friends, which would probably account for his not stopping to say hello to her and her daughters as they made their entrance. Well, this time if she had the opportunity she was going to make the grandest of impressions on him. They did know each other, after all, and her husband had been part of the court. Things were so odd in this kingdom; it never made sense to her that she hadn't been invited to court before now, or that no one had sent their regrets at Sir Richard's passing, or simply checked in to see if she and her girls were all right.

As she and her daughters stood in line waiting to be announced to the royal family, Lady Tremaine fussed over Drizella's and Anastasia's feathers and ruffles, making sure they looked perfect.

"Mother, please stop! You're making me nervous," said Anastasia, stamping her foot.

"I'm sorry, my darling. I just want you to look beautiful for the prince. I know he's going to want to marry one of you. You're the most beautiful girls here," she said, looking around the room at all the other courtly ladies and gentlemen hoping their daughters would catch the eye of the prince.

"Oh, Mother, please! You know that's not true," said Drizella. "Look at all these beautiful girls, they're all like Cinderella. We don't stand a chance." She sighed deeply.

The castle was simply bursting with eligible

young ladies, all dressed in their finest ball gowns, which glittered under the light of chandeliers. They were all breathtaking, but even Lady Tremaine had to admit to herself that none were quite as lovely as her vermin-loving stepdaughter, whom she had thankfully left back at the château.

Lady Tremaine noticed that Anastasia, too, looked self-conscious as she hid her hands, which were still cracked and dry from years of washing dishes in the kitchen.

It hurt Lady Tremaine's heart that her daughters didn't think themselves beautiful, but Sir Richard's words kept echoing in her mind again and again, making her doubt the prince would see the beauty in her daughters that she did. She wanted to protect them, and almost took them both by the hand to lead them away before they even met the prince. She wouldn't be able to bear it if the prince did anything to make her daughters feel unworthy of being there among the legion of beauties all gathered that evening. And just as she was about to take her daughters and depart, she heard a familiar voice.

"Don't leave, Lady Tremaine, not now when you finally have your chance to make a better life for yourself and your girls."

Lady Tremaine knew Rebecca's voice immediately. She wanted to rail and scream and strangle the woman for betraying her and working with those wretched witches behind her back. "Rebecca," she said calmly as Anastasia and Drizella squealed with happiness to see her.

"Hello, girls. Don't you look exquisite this evening? It's going to be some time before you and your mama will be announced and presented to court. Why don't you go get us some refreshments? You don't want to sound like croaking toads when you say hello to the prince, do you?" she said, smiling at Anastasia and Drizella.

"Oh dear! My throat is a little dry! Zella, let's go get some punch," said Anastasia. "We'll be right back!" Both girls ran off, leaving Rebecca and Lady Tremaine alone.

Lady Tremaine quickly snapped her gaze from her daughters to Rebecca. She wanted nothing more than to wrap her hands around her neck and squeeze until there was no life in her. "What are you doing here, you witch?" she asked, reaching for her brooch and speaking through clenched teeth so the other guests didn't hear them.

"So you've guessed who I am." Rebecca laughed, sounding eerily like those strange sister witches.

"Nanny told me who you are. She said you were working with the Odd Sisters. It wasn't hard to deduce you are also a witch."

Rebecca started laughing again, but this time it was joined by the laughter of others in the ballroom, and as the laughter grew, something disturbing started to happen. Everyone in the room slowed down as if they were moving through water. It was the strangest thing Lady Tremaine had ever seen. They seemed completely unaware this was happening to them. Lady Tremaine stood there watching all the guests in awe as their movements became slower and slower until finally they were all frozen in place like statues. Everyone except Lady Tremaine, Rebecca, and the Odd Sisters, who were slowly making their way toward them through the sea of statuesque party guests. Their eyes were fixed on Lady Tremaine, and she couldn't help but remember when Sir Richard had looked at her that way when they first saw each other at Lady Hackle's party. She remembered feeling like she was his prey, and that was exactly how she felt in this moment.

"Let us introduce our sister Circe," said Lucinda, or at least the one Lady Tremaine thought must be Lucinda, for she stood in the middle and spoke first.

Lucinda waved her hand, and Rebecca transformed before their eyes into a lovely golden-haired beauty with the most delicate features Lady Tremaine had ever seen. She was all silver and gold, almost luminescent, as if a light were shining from within her. As the four witch sisters stood there, Lady Tremaine couldn't help but feel bewitched by this strange group of women. It was difficult to believe the fair-haired Circe was related to the Odd Sisters. Lady Tremaine touched her brooch, wishing to slow her beating heart, willing it to stop fluttering at such a rapid rate. She needed to be calm. She needed to be confident.

"We are, all four of us, the Odd Sisters," said Circe, smiling at Lady Tremaine.

"What is the meaning of this? What have you done to everyone, and where are my daughters?"

Circe laughed. "Your daughters are quite well, Lady Tremaine. My sisters were disappointed you never summoned them for help, and now that we see you walking down the path of your own demise, we thought we would ask you one final time if we can help you."

This time it was Lady Tremaine who laughed. "Help me? Help me? You are the reason I am in this horrible place! You plotted against me and brought me here, setting all these events in motion. Your book of fairy tales marked me as a villain, *your* book, and now I am trapped within a story I can't escape." Lady Tremaine was not a violent person, but she wanted to strike this Circe. "I trusted you, and I thought you were my friend, and you betrayed me."

Circe sighed. "I am your friend, Lady Tremaine.

I have been protecting you all along. I am the one who made sure your husband found the brooch in that little shop, and I stayed by your side doing what I could to keep you safe. Didn't I have my sisters bring the tonic of your salvation, and am I not here now offering my help once again?" She tried to reach out for Lady Tremaine's hand, but Lady Tremaine recoiled from her in anger.

"Keep your hands off me, witch! I wouldn't be here if it wasn't for you and your bloody book! You are the authors of my demise! You did this!"

The four Odd Sisters laughed so hard the chandeliers swayed overhead.

"We only write what prophecy tells us, Lady Tremaine," said Circe. "We can't change what's written, but we have made it our business to try to help those who get caught in the book's tangled web. That's all we've ever wanted to do, is to help. Won't you let us now? Maybe with our magic, we can rewrite your story, but we can't do it without your permission."

It was strange for Lady Tremaine to be talking to this woman she thought was Rebecca who now looked completely different, but there was still something about Circe that felt like her old friend. For some reason she felt she could trust her even if she was just as odd as her dark-haired sisters.

"You can trust me, Lady Tremaine, I promise you," Circe said. Her sisters, Lucinda, Ruby, and Martha, smiled behind her.

"I don't know who to trust. Nanny said you cursed my brooch, is that true?"

Lucinda shook her head. "Witch and fairy magic are very different from each other. Fairies have long mistrusted witches' magic. Like you, Nanny has her own story in the book of fairy tales, and it tells us that soon she will grow to distrust the fairy magic and embrace the way of witches. But that is another story for another time."

"All of you speak in riddles! It's so confounding. Nanny said she thought you were trying to help me, but I don't understand why you would bring me here, setting all this in motion, and then offer to help me! None of it makes sense." Circe reached out for Lady Tremaine's hand once again, and this time she let the witch take it.

"Because it was written, Lady Tremaine. You were destined to come to the Many Kingdoms and marry Cinderella's father, and his abuse would turn you into a monster, causing you to abuse his daughter in turn. We thought if we could rewrite this story and make sure the brooch got into your possession, it would give you the courage to stand up to him. Don't you feel more in control when you wear it? I saw you touching it just now. That is what gave you the strength to confront me." Circe looked into Lady Tremaine's eyes.

"That's true, but why keep the book of fairy tales from me? Why stop my letters from reaching Lady Prudence?" she asked, searching Circe's face and hoping she could trust her.

"Maybe it was a mistake to keep the book from you," Circe said. "We thought it would frighten you, or perhaps lead you further down the path we were trying to help you to avoid." Lady Tremaine felt Circe was telling the truth. But before she could speak, Circe continued, "As for the letters, I'm sorry to say that was hubris. We wanted to be the ones to help you. We had countless arguments about Lady Prudence's letters, but ultimately, my sisters and I decided we wanted to be the ones who saved you, not her. Can you ever forgive me, Lady Tremaine? You must believe all we have ever wanted to do is help you and your daughters."

Lady Tremaine didn't know what to think. She desperately wanted to get her and her daughters out of the Many Kingdoms, and if trusting these treacherous witches helped them to do that, then what could possibly be the harm?

"We can help you escape, Lady Tremaine," Circe coaxed. "You don't have to marry off one of your daughters to a priggish prince. Besides, that fate lies with Cinderella."

Lady Tremaine's eyes bulged. "Cinderella? She's

not even here!" she said, looking around the ballroom. "She's at home—she—er—she has nothing to wear."

"Oh, she will be here, and the prince will want to marry her. It's all written," said Lucinda.

Lady Tremaine threw her hands up. She was sick to death of the book of fairy tales and this supposed prophecy. "If it's already written, then how do you propose we change my fate?" she asked, clutching her brooch. She felt herself growing angry. None of these women made sense. Not these witches and not Nanny.

"By magic," said the four witches at the same time, laughing again.

"But Nanny said she couldn't help me, because I am the villain in this story. How are you going to help me?" Lady Tremaine asked.

"*Her* magic can't, but ours can. The princesses are the fairies' domain," said Circe. "The villains are ours. We are the villains' fairy godmothers, if you will. Now, do you want to stand here all night while we explain how magic in the Many Kingdoms works, or do you want us to get you and your daughters back to England where you belong?"

Before Lady Tremaine could answer, a blue blur flew into the ballroom, cascading sparks. Lady Tremaine realized it was a gray-haired woman—from the looks of it, a fairy. She wore a hooded blue robe and carried a wand, the source of the sparks. The fairy looked quite a bit like Nanny, and for a brief moment, Lady Tremaine thought it might be.

"I warned you to stay away from this ballroom, Odd Sisters! I won't let you meddle with my Cinderella!" the fairy said, casting her wand at the Odd Sisters, who scattered and hid behind the frozen party guests to avoid getting spelled.

"Nanny, what are you doing?" screamed Lady Tremaine. The fairy stopped in midair and looked down at Lady Tremaine, hovering above her with an indignant look on her face.

"Oh, you must be mistaking me for my sister. She told us all about you," said the fairy. "*I'm* the

Fairy Godmother." Her expression suddenly transformed into a brilliant smile, as if saying her own name caused her great pride.

"Are you here to help me?" Lady Tremaine asked, hoping with all her heart that she was. The Odd Sisters said they wanted to help her, but something about them scared her instead. She would far prefer the help of this kindly-looking fairy in the blue robe. "Nanny said she would ask the fairies for help, but I had given up hope."

The Odd Sisters laughed mockingly, their voices screeching in the distance. "The Fairy Godmother will never help you!" they cackled.

The Fairy Godmother scanned the room, trying to figure out where their voices were coming from amid the statue-like partygoers.

"Help you?" said the Fairy Godmother in shock. "Help a villain? Don't be ridiculous. My sister, Nanny, might have been tricked into thinking you were the innocent in all this, but I'm not. I'm here to make sure nothing stands in the way of Cinderella marrying that prince, and that you and your daughters get exactly what you deserve." The fairy's shimmering wings twitched in anger.

"But Nanny said she would help me," Lady Tremaine pleaded. "She said she would see if she could talk the Fairy Council into helping me. She made a promise! You have to help me, Fairy Godmother, you just have to. You can't abandon me now."

The Fairy Godmother narrowed her eyes. "I see why my sister was so easily fooled by you. You are convincing, but even if I could help you, I wouldn't. Not after what you have done to Cinderella."

Lady Tremaine wanted to cry. She felt like she was losing her grip on reality, and she clutched her brooch for strength.

"You may not have been a villain when you landed on Morningstar shores, but you have become one since," the Fairy Godmother continued. "You have urged your daughters down the same path, encouraging them to be as nasty and miserable as you are and using them to torture my Cinderella. No, Lady Tremaine, you deserve what comes next in your story."

"What comes next? What will happen to me and my daughters?" Lady Tremaine asked, feeling as if she were trapped in some horrible nightmare where everything was upside down. She had thought she was the heroine of her own story. She had fallen in love and traveled to a foreign land to start a new life, only to realize she had been tricked. She had endured years of abuse. And now a real fairy godmother was telling her she was, in fact, not the heroine of her own tale, but the villain in someone else's. "Please tell me, what is going to happen?" she begged, grasping her brooch and willing herself to remain as calm and cold as she could be.

"You will just have to wait and see," said the Fairy Godmother, raising her wand.

"What are you doing?" asked Lady Tremaine.

"Making you forget, and setting everything back on its proper course," said the Fairy Godmother. "Oh, look, and just in time for Cinderella's arrival. I see her carriage pulling up in front of the palace now." She began to wave her wand, but the room started to rumble and shake, causing her to whirl around, searching for the source of the magic.

"Fairy Godmother, stop!" the Odd Sisters screamed, all four of them suddenly standing before the fairy and Lady Tremaine.

"Don't do this," said Circe. "We're not here to meddle with Cinderella. We're here to help Lady Tremaine. Cinderella can have her prince, just let us help Lady Tremaine and her daughters. Nanny saw what was really happening. She wanted to help the lady and her girls, but where is she now? Why has she never come back to help them?"

"My sister was sent away," the Fairy Godmother said. "I'm afraid she won't remember who she is for quite some time, let alone remember Lady Tremaine."

"You wiped her memory?" Circe was shocked.

"It was for the best. She was threatening our way of life, threatening fairy tradition. She had to be stopped," the Fairy Godmother said.

"Mark my words, Fairy Godmother," said Circe. "Your sister will be back one day, and she will take her rightful place! And we will sing and dance in the ashes when the Dark Fairy destroys the Fairylands! This, too, has been written!"

"There is no Dark Fairy, Circe. As usual you and your sisters are talking nonsense," said the Fairy Godmother.

"Oh, there will be, and one day when the stars are not right, she will destroy you for all the harm you have caused in the Many Kingdoms." The room shook as Circe spoke.

"That is enough!" The Fairy Godmother waved her wand to create a swirling vortex behind the sisters. "I told Nanny years ago we would regret setting you loose on the Many Kingdoms."

"What do you mean?" asked Lucinda, her head cocked to the side.

"Yes, what do you mean?" asked Circe, raising her hands and causing the room to shake so violently now the walls were starting to crack, and the frozen ladies and gentlemen were toppling over.

"We demand that you tell us what you mean," said all four sisters with one voice.

"Tell us now or we will destroy you!" Circe added, her eyes filled with rage.

Now it was the Fairy Godmother's turn to laugh. "Oh, please. This is my domain. You have no power over me here. We are in the princess's chapter of the story." She put her hands on her hips and had a satisfied look on her face. "I have had enough of witches. The last thing I need is to contend with the likes of you on this night of all nights. Now leave this place at once, or I will send you to Hades's domain where you belong!"

"Send us there," said Lucinda, smiling.

"I think he'd be happy to see us," said Circe, laughing.

And with that, the Fairy Godmother blasted Circe and her sisters backward into a swirling vortex.

"There!" she said with another twitch of her wand, and the vortex closed. "That was quite enough of them!"

"Where are they? What have you done with them?" cried Lady Tremaine.

The Fairy Godmother smiled. "Never you mind.

It's time to get back to your story now, dear. Let's forget this ever happened and get my Cinderella married to her prince," she said, waving her wand. At once, the ballroom sprang back into action. Anastasia and Drizella made their way back to their mother while the music played, people danced, and courtiers continued to announce each eligible maiden to the prince.

Lady Tremaine felt strange, as if she had momentarily fallen asleep. The last thing she remembered was being scolded by her daughters for fidgeting with their dresses and feathers.

"All right, my dears, I'll stop fussing. I think they are about to announce us," she said. And like that, as if she had summoned it, their names were called. As Lady Tremaine escorted her daughters to be presented before the prince, she knew this was their last chance at freedom.

The mother and her daughters curtsied before him. But instead of smiling graciously, the prince rolled his eyes, and in that moment Lady Tremaine knew in her heart that she and her daughters would be trapped in the Many Kingdoms forever.

It was then Cinderella came gliding into the ballroom, looking as if she had just stepped from the pages of a fairy tale book. All eyes in the room turned to her. Lady Tremaine hardly recognized her, and she could tell Anastasia and Drizella didn't either, but it was their stepsister who arrived just in time to steal any chances they may have had with the prince.

"Where did she get that dress?" Lady Tremaine asked through clenched teeth, watching her daughters fumble their way through their curtseys. But the prince was no longer paying attention. His eyes had moved past them, focusing only on Cinderella. Anastasia and Drizella hadn't even finished straightening up from their curtseys when he stood abruptly, making his way right past the sisters, who looked so foolish just standing there in front of the empty throne.

As Lady Tremaine watched the prince go to

Cinderella, she felt her world crumbling around her. She had lost everything. And now the girl who had betrayed her would have everything, everything Lady Tremaine had desired for herself and her own daughters. She hated Cinderella more than ever; she felt it like hot bile churning in her stomach as she stood there watching the prince kiss Cinderella's hand and then lead her to the dance floor, her silver dress gliding around her gracefully. It made Lady Tremaine sick to look at her.

This was supposed to be *her* happily ever after, and Cinderella had taken it from her. Everyone was in awe of Cinderella, crowding the edge of the dance floor, and she realized her daughters had made their way from the throne to join those clustered to see who was dancing with the prince. She didn't have it in her heart to tell them it was their stepsister. She hoped she could spare them this final humiliation at least while they were in public.

"Do we know her?" asked Drizella.

"Well, the prince certainly seems to," said Anastasia. "I know I've never seen her."

Drizella crouched down to get a better look. Lady Tremaine muttered in agreement, lying while formulating a plan to keep Cinderella from marrying the prince. She would hide her away in the basement! She thought it was a brilliant idea, and she couldn't wait to share it with her daughters once home.

As Drizella and Anastasia craned their necks to get a better look at this mysterious beauty, Lady Tremaine followed the dancing couple to the edge of the dance floor. She pretended she was also curious about the dazzling young woman with whom the prince was so smitten. As she clutched her brooch, she felt her heart grow cold and hard. And she knew what she had to do. She would make sure Cinderella would never marry the prince. If she and her daughters were going to be forced into a miserable life, then she would make sure Cinderella would, too. The girl would suffer for dashing all her dreams.

Chapter XVIII

The Unhappily Ever After

It had been many years since that fateful ball where the prince fell in love with Cinderella. The memory of that night still filled Lady Tremaine with rage. She would never forget the day Cinderella slipped her foot into the glass slipper and was spirited away to the castle to marry her prince as the entire kingdom rejoiced in celebration. Everyone, that is, except the Tremaines.

They never did escape the Many Kingdoms. As the château decayed over the years, so did Lady Tremaine's mind. We watched from our magic mirror, wishing there was something we could do to help the lady and her daughters, but the Fairy

Godmother's magic kept us from interfering. It's not often an antagonist in a fairy tale story lives to see the end of the princess's story, and we knew it must have been a misery for Lady Tremaine to know Cinderella was living a glorious life as the fair and kind queen she became.

We had hoped in those early days that we would find a way to help the lady and her daughters, but magic took us down new and unexpected paths. Like everyone else, we forgot about Lady Tremaine, tucked away as she was in a prison fashioned by fairies, locked in Cinderella's childhood home. Doomed to become crueler and more gruesome as the years passed, and how could it be otherwise? She had watched her life slip between her fingers. She had moved to another world to be with a man she thought was in love with her, only to find he was using her for her money and would trap her in her own home and make her fear for her life and for the lives of her daughters. Her whirlwind romance had turned into a nightmare.

As the years passed Lady Tremaine's mind began

to warp in its bitterness and rage. Her singular focus was getting at least one of her daughters married, all to raise them out of the squalor they had been subjected to for more years than she could recollect.

Anastasia and Drizella, too, started to change. As their mother fell deeper into madness and despair, they started to regret how they had treated Cinderella. They saw the story differently, through the eyes of young women rather than children. They would sit up in their rooms at night talking about their childhood and putting all the pieces together. They realized Cinderella wasn't being horrible to their mother as they thought in those early days; she, too, was just being controlled by her cruel and horrible father. But the most startling revelation they made in those late-night conversations was something they could never share with their mother. Besides, they had long ago stopped trying to make their mother see Cinderella's point of view. It only sent her into a fit of rage. So they kept this secret close to their hearts, and they did what their mother told them to do. They wore the white wedding gowns and listened to her ravings. It wasn't until they had grown so weary of living like wraiths in a haunted château that they finally decided to stand up for themselves. Their mother's future might be lost, but they could still fight for theirs.

It was a day like most others. It started with Lady Tremaine sitting in the dingy front parlor of her château. The room was dark, but shards of light pierced the moth-eaten curtains, making the dust and cobwebs in the room sparkle.

Their mother was ranting, and Anastasia and Drizella were doing their best to avoid her. They were in their rooms but could hear their mother's voice echoing up the stairway.

"I've ruined everything. I've ruined my life and the lives of my daughters, all for a man who only had enough love in his heart for his dead wife and his daughter."

Lady Tremaine was talking to a plump black-and-white cat who looked at her lazily as she spoke.

"We have been trapped in this house since that horrible Cinderella was spirited off by the prince and made his bride! My daughters and I should be in that castle, not that simpering fool of a girl!"

The cat blinked and continued to listen to his lady.

"She was an insane girl, talking to mice, dressing them in handmade clothing. It was disgusting! I wonder, how does the king like his queen filling the castle with grubby little mice?"

"Mother, who are you talking to?" It was Drizella. She was standing in the shadows, avoiding the blinding shards of light coming in through the moth holes of the curtains.

Lady Tremaine narrowed her eyes, trying to see her daughter. "Come into the light, my dear, so I can see you." Drizella stayed where she was. She was like a statue. She stood stock-still, too afraid to let her mother see her. "Do as I say, Zella! Do it now, and stop acting like a vampiric fool, and come into the light!" Drizella slowly inched her way out of the shadows. "I want to see all of you, girl! Not just the tips of your shoes!"

And then it became clear why Drizella was

hiding from her mother. Lady Tremaine's face turned scarlet with anger. "Ah, now I see. We've talked about this, Zella. And what did we agree upon the last time we spoke on this matter?"

"I'm never to come down those stairs without dressing properly!" said the frightened young woman.

"Precisely. Now get upstairs and change your clothes this moment!"

"Mother, please! Don't make me put that dress back on!" Drizella looked desperate, but her mother's eyes became wider as her anger grew.

"How are you going to attract a husband if you're not dressed properly?" Her booming voice sent the many black-and-white cats that populated their moldering, vine-covered château scattering. "Get upstairs and put on your dress right this moment!" Drizella looked down at her feet as her mother continued to yell. "Zella! Go! I don't want to see you again until you've changed into your dress! And send down your sister!"

The lady of the house watched her daughter disappear up the stairs.

"Foolish girl!" She threw a threadbare velvet pillow across the room. "Sorry, my dear," she said to the startled cat. "Come here, Lucifer, I'm sorry I frightened you. Come to Mommy." The cat swaggered grumpily over to his mistress. "Don't look at me like that. I said I was sorry. What are we going to do about those girls, refusing to wear their best dresses, refusing to find husbands so we can be lifted out of this squalor?"

"Mother, are you talking to the cats again?" It was Anastasia. Her ginger ringlets hung long and loose down her shoulders, framing her frightfully pale face and matching her vivid red lip paint. "You remember that isn't Lucifer, don't you? He died many years ago."

"How dare you say my sweet baby died? You aren't dead, are you, my dearest?" Lady Tremaine stroked the smug black-and-white cat, pretending to forget her daughter was there. "Don't listen to that silly girl, Lucifer. You're just fine."

"Mother, we've talked about this. He just *looks* like Lucifer."

"Stasia! How many times do I have to tell you that I've named him after his father! Now stop treating me like an addlebrained fool!" Lady Tremaine's face contorted in rage, but when she finally fixed her gaze on her daughter, the sight of Anastasia in her wedding dress seemed to snap her out of her madness. "Oh, my darling girl! Just look at you! You look so beautiful! Stasia, you will be our savior, unlike your horrible sister! Where is she? Zella! Get down here this instant!"

Drizella slowly made her way down the stairs. Her eyes were red and swollen from crying, her black eye makeup smudged. "My gods, look at you, Zella! You're beautiful!" Lady Tremaine stood up and admired both of her daughters, who now stood side by side in tattered and stained wedding dresses. They looked frightful: pale and sickly, as if their skin never saw the light of day. "Look at my precious girls! Like living dolls of perfection!"

"Mother! You can't be serious."

"What do you mean, Zella? Lucifer, do you see something wrong with the way my daughters look?"

The smug cat blinked his eyes. “See! Lucifer thinks you look beautiful! Any man who walks into this house will think you look beautiful!”

“Mother, please!” the girls said in unison. “Let us at least wash these dresses?”

Lady Tremaine turned her attention back to her cat, cooing at him and stroking his ears. “And suppose an eligible young man came to the house while your dresses were hanging to dry and you lost your chance forever? Never!” she said, returning her attentions to her cat.

“Mother! Eligible men don’t come here anymore; they haven’t for ages!” Anastasia said. “Do you know what they say about us in the village? What must Queen Cinderella think each time she hears how you act when the deliveries come from the palace!”

Lady Tremaine erupted; her anger was explosive. “Don’t you ever mention that girl’s name to me! Never! Do you understand?”

She turned her attention back down to the latest Lucifer. “Oh, my handsome man, my only love, my only companion. What will we do with these ungrateful girls? Endlessly complaining about the beautiful dresses I bought them when I still had hope they would marry and get us out of this prison. And they defend that horrible Cinderella at every opportunity!" said Lady Tremaine, still looking at her cat.

"But, Mama, if we were to appeal to Cinderella and tell her how sorry we are for everything we did, maybe she would forgive us and offer her help," said Anastasia.

"Yes, Mama, I know she would forgive us. She didn't mean to betray you, I know she didn't. She was just a child, she didn't know what she was doing," added Drizella.

Lady Tremaine's head snapped in her daughters' direction. "How dare you defend Cinderella to me! After everything she did! She is the reason we are trapped here. I won't hear her name again. I won't!" she said, returning her attention to Lucifer.

"Oh, Lucifer, what shall I do with my daughters?

I spent the last of our money on those spoiled girls, buying them the most beautiful wedding dresses, and this is how they treat me? What shall I do?"

The cat blinked and meowed in reply, and Lady Tremaine cocked her head as if she could understand him.

"What's that, Lucifer? Put the little beasts in the cellar again? I think that might just do it! That will teach them to obey their mother."

"Mother, no! Please! We won't go in the basement again! We won't!" Drizella was crying, her hands shaking with fear. "It's cold and dark down there. I won't do it!"

"You will do as I say, Drizella!" said Lady Tremaine. "You know the punishment for defending Cinderella." She grabbed Drizella by the hair, dragging her to the cellar stairs. "You dare defy me? After all I've done for you? You're as bad as Cinderella!" She pushed her daughter to the ground and held her there, taking a pair of large scissors out of her pocket. "All you two ever do is talk of Cinderella! *Cinderella this and Cinderella that! It wasn't her fault, it was her father's! Oh, Mama, we feel bad for how we treated her!* Well, I'm sick to death of it! I won't hear it anymore!"

Anastasia stood frozen as her mother held down her sister. She wanted to pull her off Drizella, but she was paralyzed with fear as her mother screamed into her sister's face.

"You're useless, the both of you! You have never been able to do anything right! You can't even wear the dresses I bought you! *Oh, Mama, we look horrible. Can't we please take off these dirty dresses?* If you think you look horrible now, just you wait until I am finished with you!"

To Anastasia's horror, Lady Tremaine started hacking away at Drizella's ringlets.

"Traitor!" she screeched, over and over. "You don't think I know your dirty little secrets, the ones you whisper in the dark of night? Do you think I'm a fool? How else would Cinderella have known we were planning to leave if you hadn't told her? You all betrayed me!" she bellowed as she hacked off more of her daughter's hair.

"Mother, no!" said Anastasia as she tried to pull her mother off her sister, but Lady Tremaine swung back at her, slicing her arm with the scissors. Anastasia screamed, recoiling in fear and horror as she watched Drizella struggling to free herself.

CHAPTER XIX

HAPPILY EVER AFTER

"That is enough!" said the Fairy Godmother, closing the book. "I can't read anymore. Nanny, you're right. We have to get those girls out of that house."

The other fairies agreed.

"Yes! Please, go at once. The Good Fairies and I will watch over the Fairylands while you're gone!" said the Blue Fairy.

"Yes, Fairy Godmother, go!" chimed in Merryweather. "Before that horrendous woman kills them. She's gone mad. I had no idea things were so bad for them."

"Those poor girls!" screeched Flora.

"Oh, I feel just terrible for them. Maybe we should all go," added Fauna.

"Thank you, my good fairies, but I think Nanny and I should handle this on our own. That is, if she will agree to go with me," the Fairy Godmother said, looking at her sister.

"Yes, of course I will help you, my sister," Nanny agreed. "I feel we both owe it to Anastasia and Drizella for not protecting them when we should have."

"I agree, but I refuse to help their mother. She's a beastly, horrible woman," said the Fairy Godmother.

"I agree," said Nanny. "But you know as well as I do it's our fault she's turned out this way. I should have gone against the council and helped her back then, before everything fell apart."

To her surprise, her sister agreed. "You know, I never thought I would hear myself say this, but I think the Odd Sisters were actually trying to help Lady Tremaine," said the Fairy Godmother.

"Yes, I do believe you're right. It's a shame they

always seem to find a way to make it go all wrong," said Nanny.

⚜ ⚜ ⚜ ⚜

After sending Cinderella a note to reassure her they would help her stepsisters, the Fairy Godmother and Nanny took to the sky and flew right over Cinderella's old home. The château was covered in vines and crumbling from neglect and decay. As they landed in the yard, the Fairy Godmother's heart felt sick. She had done this. It was her own fairy magic that had trapped those girls in this house with their terrible mother, squandering their youth. Now that she had read what Lady Tremaine was capable of doing to her own daughters, she didn't regret what she had done to the woman. But Anastasia and Drizella deserved better. And she was about to make amends. She just hoped it wasn't too late.

"I feel terrible, too," said Nanny, reading her sister's mind. "I should have protected them. I should have been their fairy godmother. And I should have helped their mother before it was too late."

The Fairy Godmother put her arm around her sister. "You couldn't, dear. You were fairy-bound by another mission, and let's not forget you lost your memory. I should have told you what became of the Tremaines when you returned to the Fairylands. If this is anyone's fault, it's mine. But we're making it up to them now. And because of you, from now on the fairies will extend their reach beyond would-be princesses, just as you have always wished. This story has finally shown me that you have been right all along," she said, giving her sister a kiss on the cheek.

"Oh, sister, do you mean it?" asked Nanny.

The Fairy Godmother laughed. "Do I have a choice? You're ruling the Fairylands now."

"Well, no, I suppose you don't have a choice, but I'm so happy I will have you at my side," Nanny said.

"Okay, enough of this talk, we have a job to do," said the Fairy Godmother, taking her wand from her sleeve. She was wearing her billowing blue hooded robe, the one she had worn when she helped

Cinderella all those years ago. It was fitting, really. She had come full circle. "And our work is cut out for us, look at the state of this place!" she said, gesturing to indicate the château.

"Oh, we have repaired worse, my sister. We rebuilt the Fairylands and Morningstar Kingdom after they were destroyed by Maleficent. I think we can handle this," Nanny said, taking her sister by the hand as they walked up to the front door.

They could see Anastasia and Drizella peeking at them through the basement windows. They looked ghastly. It was no wonder people of the village thought they were ghosts. And everywhere they looked there were black-and-white cats and kittens of various sizes roaming around, meowing grumpily at the fairies.

"Shall we knock or just go right in?" Nanny asked.

"I say we knock, no sense in being rude," said the Fairy Godmother.

But before they could do so, the door opened violently to reveal Lady Tremaine's wrathful face.

"I have already told you I am not interested in

your witchery! Stay away from my house!" screamed Lady Tremaine.

The Fairy Godmother was shocked. "Well, that's a first, being mistaken for a witch." The Fairy Godmother ruffled her wings. "We are not witches, lady, but fairies of the highest order! Now let us in or we will be forced to use our magic."

But Lady Tremaine kept railing on them. "I don't care if you're witches, fairies, or Hades himself, I will not allow you in my house! I remember you from the ball. And do you think I don't remember you, too, Nanny? How dare you come here with your witch sister after all these years, after denying my pleas for help. How dare you let my daughters and me rot away in this squalor! Why are you here? To finally take my brooch? Well, you can't have it! It's mine, and I won't part with it! My husband gave it to me. The only person who has ever truly loved me. And I won't give it up. I won't."

"We are so sorry for how this turned out, Lady Tremaine, truly, and we want to make amends.

May we come in? We would like to help you and your daughters. We understand they are down in the cellar. Won't you please let us bring them out into the light and give them a better life?" Nanny searched the angry woman's face for something of the woman she once knew. But all she saw was anger, heartbreak, and betrayal. A cold heart.

She was beyond helping, beyond saving.

"So, you have been using your magic to spy on me? Using your vile witchery! Do you think I'm an addled old fool? I will never let you have my daughters! Everything I've ever done, I've done for them! Everything! What do you plan to do, let them go? And what will become of me?" she asked, advancing on the fairies wielding a long pair of bloodstained scissors, slicing at the air and screaming.

"That is enough out of you!" said the Fairy Godmother, blasting Lady Tremaine with her magic wand.

Lady Tremaine vanished into thin air.

"What happened to her? What did you do

with her?" asked Nanny, looking around for Lady Tremaine.

"I'll tell you later. Now we have to get those girls out of the cellar," the Fairy Godmother said, using her wand to burst open the door.

"Girls! You can come out now, it's safe," said the Fairy Godmother. Then slowly and tentatively, two frail, dingy-looking young women came creeping out of the cellar. They looked like frightened wraiths. Their hair had been cut off in random hanks, and their faces were heavily swollen with long hours of crying.

"Are you here to help us?" said Anastasia as she came out, her sister, Drizella, hiding behind her. "Like you helped Cinderella?"

"Yes, dears, we're here to help you. We're just sorry it took us so long," said the Fairy Godmother. She waved her wand, restoring each girl's lovely ringlets.

"Can you ever forgive me?" the Fairy Godmother asked, taking both girls in her arms.

"Are you our fairy godmother?" asked Drizella.

"We wished for you to come every day," Anastasia said.

"Yes, we both are," said Nanny. "And we have a message for you from the queen."

"Oh, Nanny, it's you! You came back for us. We hoped you would. We missed you so much!" said Drizella, causing tears to prick Nanny's eyes.

"I'm sorry it took me so long to find my way back to you, girls. I hope one day we can sit together and I will tell you the story, and I hope with all my heart you will forgive me," she said, hugging them.

"Nanny, did you say the queen had a message for us? Queen Cinderella? She sent you here?" said Anastasia.

"Yes, my dear. She sent us here to help you," said the Fairy Godmother.

"And she is holding a ball in your honor, to welcome you to court. She has invited every eligible gentleman to attend," said Nanny.

But both girls started to cry.

"What's the matter?" asked the Fairy Godmother. "Why are you crying?"

"Well, look at us! We can't go to the palace looking like this. And who says we want to attend a ball, or even want to marry?" said Drizella.

"The choice is yours, of course," Nanny said.

"Oh, but surely you'd like to see your sister," Fairy Godmother cut in, "and then you can decide if you'd like to stay there with her, or come back to live here. It's entirely up to you."

"I think I would like to go back home to England after we tell Cinderella how sorry we are for everything that happened," said Anastasia.

"I would, too. But how can we? And how can we possibly face Cinderella after what we did to her?" Drizella added through tears.

"Oh, my dear girl," said the Fairy Godmother. "Cinderella said something to me many years ago, on her wedding day. She said she understood why you and your mother hated her. At the time I didn't understand. But after reading your story, I think now I do."

"Do you really think she will forgive us?" asked Anastasia.

"Oh, my darling girl, she already has," said Nanny. "And I hope you will find it within your hearts to forgive her," she added, taking both of the girls' hands.

"Oh, Nanny!" said Anastasia. "We really have missed you." She hugged the old woman again. "But we can't go to the castle like this!"

"Well, dears, that's what you have fairy godmothers for!" said the Fairy Godmother, winking at Nanny.

"Oh, I know you want to sing the bibbidi-bobbidi-boo song! Go on, then!" said Nanny.

The Fairy Godmother was happier than she had been in years. Singing her magical words and waving her wand, granting wishes, and setting things right, but this time it was with her sister,

Nanny. She had dreamed one day they would do magic like this together, and finally her dream had come true. And before they both knew it, the entire house was made beautiful again, as it had been years before. Just like that.

"Now, girls, we completely understand if you don't wish to live here, but you're welcome to, of course. Cinderella says the house is yours. But just say the word and we will arrange another place for you to stay, or send you back to England. We will carry out your wishes," said the Fairy Godmother, eyeing the royal carriage that had just arrived.

Anastasia and Drizella stood in amazement.

"Come along, girls, there is a carriage to take you to see your sister at the royal palace. She is waiting for you." The Fairy Godmother ushered the girls toward the carriage.

"But . . ." said Drizella.

"But nothing. Cinderella is very excited to see you," she said, pushing them to the carriage door.

"But, Fairy Godmother," said Anastasia, "we're not dressed properly."

"Oh yes, the dress. I always forget," said the Fairy Godmother with a laugh, remembering how she had almost forgotten Cinderella's dress until the very last moment all those years ago. "Nanny, would you like to do the honors this time?" she asked.

"It would be my pleasure," said Nanny, conjuring beautiful gowns for Anastasia and Drizella. The Fairy Godmother could tell her sister was enjoying fairy-craft—she was in her element really—and it made her smile to see her happy again after everything she had gone through with her other charges. The two fairies stood back, admiring their handiwork, and they thought Lady Tremaine was right: her daughters were beautiful. They looked so lovely in their gowns. Anastasia's was a voluminous crimson dress with an elaborate golden brocade, and Drizella was wearing one in eggplant with silver embellishments. They were stunning.

"Now then, you two look perfect. Absolutely beautiful," said the Fairy Godmother.

"Oh really, Fairy Godmother? Do we really?" asked Anastasia.

"Oh yes, my dears," she said right before the girls enveloped her and Nanny in hugs and kisses.

"Thank you so much!" they said as one, stepping into the carriage.

"No, wait, we forgot one thing," the Fairy Godmother said, shooting sparks at both of their feet. "We mustn't forget the glass slippers!" she said. "Now you truly are perfect! Oh yes, and here is your royal invitation." She handed it to Anastasia. "Be sure to show it to the guards when your carriage arrives to the castle. And please tell Cinderella how much I love her."

"Aren't you coming with us?" asked Drizella.

"Oh, no, dear, we plan to fill your closets with lovely clothes and figure out what to do with all these cats! There's still work to be done here. Don't worry, Cinderella will take good care of you. And if you ever need anything at all, please just make a wish upon a star, and I promise you this time we will appear," said the Fairy Godmother.

Both Anastasia and Drizella kissed their fairy godmothers on their cheeks.

"Go on now, you don't want to keep your sister waiting," Nanny said with tears in her eyes. "And don't worry, these enchantments won't ever break. Your coach won't turn into a pumpkin," she said, laughing.

"But, Fairy Godmother, what happened to our mother? Will she be back?" asked Drizella from the carriage.

Fairy Godmother smiled at the girls. "Don't you worry about her, girls. I promise you she will never hurt you again. Now off with you, to the palace! Nanny and I have important things to do!" she said as Anastasia and Drizella's carriage drove away, Anastasia and Drizella waving and smiling at their fairy godmothers.

"Goodbye, girls. Have a lovely time at the palace," called the Fairy Godmother as she watched it ride away.

"I'm very proud of you, sister," said Nanny, hugging the Fairy Godmother. "By the way, what *did* you do with Lady Tremaine?"

"I'll show you," the Fairy Godmother said with

an impish smile on her face. "She is exactly where she belongs. I almost put her down in the basement," she said, leading Nanny up to Cinderella's old attic bedroom. "But I decided the attic would be better."

Nanny couldn't help but gasp. There in the middle of the room was Lady Tremaine, forever frozen in time, her hand at her brooch, and her cat, Lucifer, curled up at her feet.

"You've turned her into a statue?" said Nanny.

"Yes," said the Fairy Godmother, chuckling as she noticed that some mice had made a nest in Lady Tremaine's hair.

At last, Lady Tremaine was cold, solid, and unmovable, as she had always wished.

THE END